The Partisan

and other stories

Other story collections published by Evertype

The Partisan and other Stories (Gabriel Rosenstock,
tr. Mícheál Ó hAodha & Gabriel Rosenstock 2014)

The Book of Poison (Panu Petteri Höglund & S. Albert Kivinen,
tr. Colin Parmer & Tino Warinowski 2014)

*Neighbours: Stories in Mennonite Low German and English
Nohbasch: Jeschichte in Plautdietsch und Englisch*
(Jack Thiessen 2014)

The Burning Woman and other stories (Frank Roger 2012)

The Partisan

and other stories

By

Gabriel Rosenstock

evertype

2014

Published by Evertype, Cnoc Sceichín, Leac an Anfa, Cathair na Mart, Co. Mhaigh Eo, Éire. www.evertype.com.

First edition 2014.

A catalogue record for this book is available from the British Library.

ISBN-10 1-78201-057-2
ISBN-13 978-1-78201-057-9

Set in Dutch Mediaeval and Imprint MT Shadow by Michael Everson.

Cover by Michael Everson, after the painting *Partizánka na stráži pod Rozsutcom* by Ján Mudroch, 1954.

Printed by: LightningSource.

Contents

Acknowledgements

"...everything emptying into white..." appeared in Irish in *Comhar* magazine under the title "Lipica". A version in English appeared in *Irish Pages*; it was subsequently anthologized in *Best European Fiction 2012* (Dalkey Archive Press).

"Dearcán" appeared in *The Stinging Fly*, issue 9, 2001.

"The Khrushchëv shoe" first appeared in Irish as the title story of *Bróg Khruschev agus scéalta eile* (Cló Iar-Chonnachta, 1998) and later in English in the anthology *Twisted Truths* (Cló Iar-Chonnachta, 2011), ed. Brian Ó Conchubhair, introduced by Colm Tóibín.

"Hermit" first appeared in Irish in *Bróg Khruschev* under the title "An Díthreabhach".

"King of the Jungle" first appeared in Irish as "Rí na Dufaire" in *Bróg Khruschev*.

"Lost in Translation" was first published in Irish as "Aigne i gCéin" in *Bróg Khruschev*.

"What else would the son of a cat do?" was first published in Irish in the monthly magazine, *Feasta*, as "Cad a dhéanfadh mac an chait..."

"Kaddish" first appeared in Irish in *Bróg Khruschev*.

"Bird Clan" was first published as one of two long short stories in book *Clann na nÉan/Rí na Cailce* (Comhar, 2005)

"The Partisan" and "The silent swish-swish of Dust Blowers" appear here for the first time, and "Hermit", "King of the Jungle", "Lost in Translation", "What else would the son of a cat do?", "Kaddish", and "Bird Clan" all appear here in English for the first time.

The Partisan

and other stories

"…everything emptying into white…"

She herself was from Lipica. Lipica of the countless caves and souterrains. And the snobbish white horses. If one could put it like that.

Sure, they have airs and graces. But only when they perform. Left to their own devices and they were perfectly fine.

"Born black, I understand?"

She nodded impassively. Tired of answering the same old questions, was she? I made a mental note not to ask too many questions. Her response was dismissive.

"As black as your Aesop! Can't say I'm terribly interested in them. They are so clichéd, aren't they? Like yourselves and the leprechauns."

I let it pass. Lipizaners and leprechauns. Tenuous. That was another good word, that. A word that described much of what we had heard during the conference, truth be told.

It was my first time in Slovenia. And Miljana – that was her name – she was my minder. I would have been happy enough to remain alone (I think) but we lecturers were each assigned a personal assistant. Some of them were more of a nuisance than a help, really. Mentioning the horses was just my way of passing the time. Small talk. Talk for the sake of talk. For someone who earns his living by talking, maybe I wasn't so good at it really. Not unless I was rattling on about folkloric motifs. The water nymph and the veil. Greek legends. Comparisons with similar myths and legends concerning mermaids and kelpies in Ireland

and Scotland. *Compare and contrast the sexual tropes in Greek myths and Irish tales concerning mermaids and nymphs.*

Yes, yes! Yes, you will give me back my veil, yes you will, but not before you have learned to love me more than any man has ever loved before. Then, and not until then, will you give me back my veil so that I may join my sisters again, nymphs immortal as rivers.

"If you wish, of course, we can go and have a look at them after the conference."

Nymphs? What? Oh, the horses.

"I'm quite content to watch them from my window. They fill me with calm."

That is true. As they grazed I felt a sense of peace wash over me. But then one or two of them decided to trot around the field, flicking their tails, only to return more or less to the same spot, rubbing one neck against the other, and my sense of calm waned.

Miljana looked at me curiously. She had long, golden hair. Mane-like. Her white body, it was paler than the Lipizaners.

"And strength," I added, returning to the horses. "They fill me with strength."

(True. And yet sometimes they drain me of everything.)

"Strength? Might it not be all in your imagination?" Hard to detect from her tone if this observation was ironic or not. Myths and legends, and their origins, that's my field. Yes, but that doesn't mean I believe in fairy horses. Like most scholars, I'm a rationalist. I don't know if I ever met a colleague who ~ that's not quite correct. Finlay, from Edinburgh. He went a bit funny in the end, didn't he?

She kicked some leaves that had gathered together on the gravel path. Idly. Without malice. Yet, with intent?

"Judging by the paper you read yesterday, you must have some imagination!"

I was slowly warming to her. She was trying to be friendly. Informal. That was her function after all.

"Know something about ancient Greek fables then, do we?" I asked, teasingly.

"Well, I do now, thanks to your paper. I had forgotten ~ if I ever knew it ~ that Aesop was black. Is your room OK?"

"It's fine." I didn't know what else to say. The bed is a bit lumpy? Sheets slightly damp? Wall-paper old-fashioned. The prints on the wall, the romantic sunsets. The view from the window compensates for any defects. Something like that? But I wasn't fast enough. I rarely am. Scholars think slowly, after all. I kicked some leaves as if by repeating her earlier action we would, somehow, have a connection. The leaves were dead. They had already turned black and mushy.

3

We were taking the air. Literally. I was trying to scoop as much of it as I could into my lungs. A little break before lunch. A stroll. A stretching of the limbs. I would have preferred to be alone but Miljana had her job to do. She was my shadow. She was not allowed to let me out of her sight until she had shovelled me on to that return flight in Trieste. They had "lost" a lecturer at last year's conference and it wasn't going to happen again. The man's wife had phoned the day after the conference had ended. Where was Roberto? Why hadn't he come home? A heart attack? Had he gone off with the fairies? (The man was a world authority on Persian fairy tales.)

In the distance, I watched a youth dismount from his bicycle. In full racing regalia, he stepped towards a fig tree, reached up and gently dislodged a fig. He ate it slowly and with relish, then wiped the juice from his mouth, mounted his bike and cycled away. It was as though the world was his and his alone. He was all in blue. A modern, athletic version of *The Blue Boy*.

I inhaled deeply.

"The air is good here," I remarked.

"You don't have good air in Ireland?"

I looked at her. I wanted to say that the air was drier here but instead I just smiled. Somewhat sheepishly. Ten yards from where we were standing, a small apple that had been squashed underfoot on the road. A crow was gorging itself on it. It looked around every so often at a jealous magpie who was also eyeing up the juicy prize. *The crow, the blackbird, and the raven in Irish and Welsh folklore. Discuss.*

"You remind me of someone," she said.

I do?

"France Prešeren, our national poet."

Really? I wanted to ask, but didn't. I knew next to nothing about Prešeren but one thing I did know is that no portrait of him existed anywhere, not even the vaguest of likenesses.

Just then – the sound of the gong. Our time-keeper had appeared again, like an innkeeper from a Hammer horror film. Eight times the harridan struck that gong, unflinchingly. Twice was more than enough. We made our way towards the dining hall, Miljana, my shadow, preceding me. For a minute, I felt that both of us were prisoners in a strange drama.

I had hoped that our little stroll would have done something for my appetite. It hadn't. Time to open the communication lines again. It was good manners if nothing else. I glanced at her left breast and her name tag: Miljana Mahkota. I already knew that. Why had I done a double take? She could hardly change her name overnight, could she?

It always takes me a day or two to adjust to a new environment. New accents. New surroundings. The air. The light. All of it. The bed. Pillows. How some people made such transitions so smoothly was a wonder to me. How did they do it? Six weeks previously I had given up smoking and this had made me a little fidgety. I wasn't sure now what to do with my right hand. The loss of the familiar cigarette left me bereft. It was, I imagined, akin to the loss of a limb.

No, there was also something else amiss. Something I was unable to put a finger on.

"Well, Miljana. Do you do this often?"

"What? Eat lunch?"

I gave a small laugh.

"Actually, you're my first!" she grinned and lifted a grey napkin. She shook it out, as one might shake out a sheet.

5

Reverently she covered her lap with it. At least, it struck me as an act of reverence. Self-reverence.

"This is just a part-time job for me. I used to work for a film club in Ljubjlana, for about four and a half years. Then the founder died and things were never the same again. Something disappeared and was lost forever. A vision. Know what I mean?"

"I suppose," I said, lamely.

"It's hard to explain. The vision died with him." She looked into the distance, searching for a word. A word in her own language, maybe? Somehow I sensed that I would never hear that word from her lips.

"I understand," I said, pressing the bread roll for freshness. "Are you interested in film?" I asked.

"I was for a while," she replied.

She must have loved that person. The one with the vision. Yes, that's it, I said to myself, pleased with my discovery. Soup was served. Vegetable soup. It needed salt. But I had been told to cut back on salt.

"We were living on air in those days," she remarked, tasting the soup.

I had no idea what she meant and she must have noticed the puzzled expression on my face.

"We were still a new nation then. We wanted to taste everything, especially anything that was forbidden. Books, music, film ~ everything." She sprinkled salt on her soup.

"Of course," I said. "One forgets about such things. I read something recently, a newspaper report. The film censor in Sweden said that they should get rid of his job, that they have no need of him anymore. Adults should be allowed to look at anything they want."

"I ~"

Her response was interrupted by an announcement that the final session would commence at two o'clock. Why the announcement? We all had the programme and everything had run like clockwork so far. I lifted a spoon, mindlessly, and saw myself in it, distorted, a monster from Tibetan folklore. Maybe this is me. Or maybe it's Prešeren? The elusive France Prešeren, tracked down at last. I returned the magic spoon to its place. There was something about this dining room that unnerved me. It might have suited soldiers once. Or monks even. There was no sign of the feminine touch anywhere. The grey napkins, coarse and uninviting to the touch. Maybe there were still places in Slovenia that preferred to look back, people for whom the great leap towards apparent freedom was all too much.

The main course was a choice of pork or fish. We both had the fish. She seemed concerned about the bones. I asked her what kind of fish it was we were tasting but she couldn't think of the English equivalent. Was it caught locally? She didn't know that either.

We spoke little for the rest of the meal. I couldn't get last night's dream out of my head. I was in a coach, on my own. It was the era of the Austro-Hungarian Empire and I was somebody of some minor importance. The horses were Lipizaners. I was reading Heinrich Heine. I turned a page and casually looked out from where I was sitting. The horses had sprouted wings. We were flying.

* * *

"You didn't like?" she asked.

I had only eaten half of my lunch and what remained was cold and shapeless.

"It was fine, thanks," I answered. "Not very hungry."

"I suspect you spend too much time stuck in books. You should get out more often."

"So my doctor tells me."

7

It was then that I noticed how astonishingly healthy she looked. All over. Her hair. Her eyes. Her teeth. Gums. Everything. Even her fingernails had a hint of perfection about them.

"Coffee?"

I said yes.

Neither of us bothered with dessert. She alluded again to my lecture.

"So, Alexander's soldiers brought dozens of tales back with them from India, tales which would influence European storytelling for centuries. You may not have noticed it, but your theories annoyed quite a few people yesterday."

"Goodness, why?" I hadn't noticed. I'm slow to pick up on such things.

"Well, some of my fellow Slovenians in particular, I have to say." She glanced briefly to her left and right.

"Go on." I was curious. I couldn't recall a previous occasion in which a paper of mine had been a source of annoyance. Boredom, yes. But annoyance. Hardly.

She licked some foam from her lower lip.

"You see, we're not in Yugoslavia anymore. We're all Europeans now and ~ purely on an unconscious level, you understand ~ some of us don't like anything that might diminish our sense of Europe's importance. If Aesop is more Indian than Greek, as you claim, well that's one small chipping away at the foundations of European culture and we won't buy it. I buy it but many right-wing bastards are on the move again. Had you said Aesop was influenced by the Irish, that would have been tolerable enough. The Irish are white. But India? Now, that's a horse of a different colour."

I exhaled deeply. Bastards? Hadn't expected that word from her pristine lips.

"I didn't intend that people should take my lecture personally."

She raised an eyebrow. How well she did that small gesture of hers. What films did they show in that film club of hers? Maybe she had studied them? *Casablanca*?

"Isn't everything personal?"

You think so?

I shrugged. That was the extent of my response.

The eyebrow was still raised in that inscrutable fashion of hers, maybe expecting a better answer from me.

"This conversation is personal, isn't it?"

I thought about this for a second or two.

"No it's not..."

She's confident almost to the point of cockiness, this lady. Well, she belongs to a different generation, doesn't she? What is she, twenty, twenty five years younger than I am?

"Am I in love with my wife? Now, had you asked me that, our conversation would have been personal."

"And are you?" she shot back.

People had begun to disperse, now. There was the sound of chairs and laughter. Conversations in German, Croatian, French, English, and Slovene. Lecturers, minders and a host of other functionaries all taking their circuitous routes back to the lecture hall. My name tag was askew, so I straightened it and stood up. I closed the middle button of my jacket. My weight had fluctuated a lot in the past six months but the jacket still closed easily enough. I sat down again as I felt a sudden dizziness. Had I forgotten to take the blood pressure tablets?

"Feeling OK?" Her voice came to me as if from a distance.

I took a swig of water; it revived me. After a little while I stood up. She offered me her arm.

9

"What happened to your man anyway?" I asked.

"Who?"

"The lecturer who never made it home."

"Oh! Roberto. The trouble he caused! They found him in that big cave, the one in Vilenicia, you've been there, haven't you?. Three days and three nights spent underground. The poor man didn't know if he was coming or going."

I tried to imagine his ordeal.

"We needn't go back to the lecture hall," she suggested.

We were the last two people in the refectory now, other than the staff.

It was my turn to raise an eyebrow.

"We could go and look at the Lipizaners, if you like."

That was all of four years ago. I never saw her again. I was briefly reminded of her by an item on television about the Lipizaners. Don't ask me what it was about. I didn't hear the commentary, transfixed as I was by the horses. Dancing. Prancing. Leaping out of their skins.

~ Translated from the Irish by the author

10

The Partisan

It had to be a Kalashnikov, I said to myself. I was guessing. I don't know anything about weapons but Kalashnikovs I had heard of. And there she was in front of me, a rifle firmly in her grasp, raised, but not aimed at me, the strap coming down over her right breast. Red lips matching a red kerchief. How much blood has she spilled? The eyes say nothing. Is she totally brainwashed? (She asks me the same question. Touché!) Nor did her full lips show any feeling either. Lips, too, can betray feelings as much as eyes – or lack of feeling. I look at her hands again. Terribly difficult to get right, they say, but Ján Mudroch got it right. Except that they look like the hands of a man. What do you expect, lugging a Kalashnikov over hill and dale. And from the vague, misty background she appears to be in mountainous territory. On the run? Dressed for warmth. She doesn't look hungry. Has she shot and skinned a rabbit and eaten it? Her hair lacks lustre. How long since she washed it? The thousand and one items that women have today to prettify themselves – eye-liners, moisturisers, toners, anti-wrinkle creams and the devil knows what else, she has none of these. Nor does she need them. She has the mountain air.

No catalogue (or had I decided not to buy one?) so I took out my smartphone and looked him up but foolishly wrote Ján Murdoch – instead of Mudroch – and if such a person exists at all he's done nothing to deserve an entry. Believing the artist to be some poor forgotten genius, I mumbled an obscenity and cursed our cruel world.

So, there I was, staring at this woman with a Kalashnikov. Mudroch's woman must have struck the curators, too, as an iconic image as she adorns the cover of a notebook that I bought on my way out. The title of the painting is in Slovak: *Partizánka na stráži pod Rozsutcom*. I guessed that *partizánka* meant "partisan". I could have looked for a computer translation but I didn't. I don't know why. Maybe I didn't want a full explanation. Not knowing who she was, or what exactly she was up to, satisfied me in a peculiar way. The mystery magnetized me to her. Was she real? A real fighter, a real partisan, a real woman? Was that a real Kalashnikov? Or a prop? Did Murdoch or Mudroch or whatever his name was, did he paint the woman in a studio? Was she his wife, or daughter? The girl next door? What does it mean, to be a partisan? Who was she fighting? Germans? What was she fighting for? Slovakian independence? I was harbouring doubts about the rifle. More of a blunderbuss than a Kalashnikov. A heavy, awkward-looking thing. But what do I know about rifles, about anything?

No, she couldn't be the girl next door. Look at that nose, the jaw line, the neck. The whole stance. She's a peasant. A fearless peasant fighter. I want to be on her side. By her side. What was all that business a long time ago, before I was born, something to do with Americans methodically destroying the reputation of Soviet artists, undermining social realism by investing millions in non-figurative, abstract art. Hundreds of women, like my woman with the Kalashnikov, thousands like her never came to be, never reached the canvas.

She, my Kalashnikov woman, was a dying breed along with all the other men and women who laboured in steel factories or rode tractors in endless fields of wheat. Their days numbered. Outflanked, out-manoeuvred, by CIA dollars and lackey art critics. And do I spend long hours looking at Pollock's squiggles and blobs and smears? No, I don't. Bird droppings! But I did spend time looking at the woman with the Kalashnikov. And still do. What were her dreams and hopes? Were they ever realized?

She could be any age. Eighteen? Twenty five? Every time I look at her I ask myself, is it with full and utter conviction that she makes her stand, with faith and undying determination? Or has she doubts? Is she afraid, desperate even? Is she, so to speak, out of the picture? Has she any idea of what her role might be in the larger scheme of things?

I had found myself in Bratislava, no longer knowing if I myself belonged to a larger scheme of things or not. Perhaps not, I concluded. I wasn't prepared for the rain and it was rain that had brought me into the gallery. I looked at dozens of pictures. A portrait of Gorki. Jews in a ghetto, one of them about to topple out of the picture frame, into oblivion. But it was my partisan with the Kalashnikov that wooed me. Wooed me, did I say? Oh no, she is not trying to woo me or win me or anybody like me. Me? I don't exist for her. I don't deserve her, her Kalashnikov raised, at the ready. Even her chin seems to say she is determined to fight, fight to the death. And if I get in her way she'll mow me down.

Why did I ever doubt her, if only for a moment? Perhaps I've led a sheltered existence, but I have never seen a woman holding a rifle or a gun, never even knew a woman who owned a firearm. How did Jackson Pollock die? With a gun? No, alcohol, if I remember correctly, and a car accident.

When I got home, I found that I was unable to forget her. It was her aloneness that got to me. Haunted me. Where were her compatriots? Dead? Impossible as it may sound, she ceased to be an obscure part of history, frozen in time.

More and more, she began to invade the present, insinuating herself into my life. Coming alive. Those flesh tones were not the work of an amateur. Yes, I eventually caught up with the elusive Mudroch and his works but even his nudes, though beautifully executed, were of no interest to me. She alone seemed to be making a meaningful statement. In what way "meaningful" I could not explain, to myself or others. Actually, there were no others. My wife picked up the notebook one day and idly asked, "Writing again?" She knew from the feel of it that the notebook was unused; and as for the unfashionable image that stares out boldly from the cover, how on earth could she have known that it was taking over my life?

My wife is far too busy looking after her favourite aunt to bother much about my bungling goings on and never lets an opportunity pass without reminding me that her beloved aunt has "old money", money that will soon be ours. The way she says "old money" makes it sound respectable, giving it a patina so that it has become like some valued object seen on the Antiques Road Show. Old money! Fall out of the sky, did it? More likely out of Africa or India.

I downloaded the painting. It's my screensaver now. It has replaced a sunset image of a lake on which snow geese were resting, others departing or coming in. It wasn't a Kalashnikov at all ~ shows you how much I know! ~ but a machine gun, a PPSh-41. It's not that difficult to get your hands on one, you know. They made six million of them after all! I have my own one now. And ammo galore to go with it. I was angry with myself, fuming in fact, that I hadn't known the difference between a Kalashnikov rifle and a PPSh-41. How scornful she would be! But whatever else I'm going to do, this much is certain: I'm going to earn her respect, her trust, her love. As a partisan.

I drive up to the mountains most Saturdays and Sundays and trudge along lonely, narrow, briar-bordered paths, alert, on the lookout, as she is, and you'd swear I was carrying a machine gun all my life! Sometimes I stand, motionless, and look down on the city, holding the weapon the way she does, at the same angle. I look and I stare, just as she does. What was her dream? It's still alive, isn't it? It has to be. I live it now, for her. For everybody. And I listen to the meadow pipit. Listen long enough and it sounds like rapid gun-fire.

Dearcán

The dull-eyed doe
drinks not in dale or dingle.
Doves dumb.
Dogs howl their dirges
in the distance:
Dry dreams
of dastardly men...
(desunt cetera)

Dearcán (c. 317 ~ 340)

Dere once was a Druid who lived in a dank dwelling known as *Doire an Draoi,* de Oak-grove of de Druid. He liked to dabble in dis and dat. His name was Dearcán which, as everyone knows, means an acorn, or pig-berry, or possible de head of a tistle ~ dough he himself favoured anoder derivation, and a dubious one at dat ~ de dear little mote in de dawn sunbeam.

Dearcán was a dab hand at spells, magic, alchemy, and had cures for all sorts of tings, including de dreaded dysentery. Daffodils he adored. It's said he invented de daisy-chain.

Now, de people feared him dough it was common knowledge dat he was daft. He smoked various carefully detoxed herbal mixtures in a dainty if slightly damaged chalk-pipe, a *dúidín,* including a dirty substance he called "dagga" which was said to contain de dried droppings of dormice.

18

His diet consisted of nuts, watercress, dulse, salmon, dandelions, oats, and barley but he denied himself all dairy produce. He was someting of a dandy, was our Dearcán, in de matter of dress, demeanour and daily hygiene. His remedy for dandruff was an oily substance extracted from de bark of birch trees on designated, dark, December nights. A practical dude in some respects, he darned his own drawers wit' his eyes shut.

Neider son nor daughter did Dearcán have to dote upon, not surprising as he had never dallied wit' or desired a damsel (wit' or wit'out a dulcimer). His days were doleful, his nights dreary, his career short-lived but dazzling all de same. He knew de day and de hour of his demise.

Dearcán was slightly deaf in one ear, which does explain his declamatory ~ some would say demonic ~ style of oratory. Dozens of doughty dopes came from miles around to observe him dandering *deasil*, clockwise, around his deambulatory. Dey followed him in droves when he wandered abroad to view a debacle, say ~ de breaking up of distressed ice on a river was deemed a distinguished omen ~ or to study his deliberations as he duly cocked his good ear to de dreadful declamations of de wild duck dissembling over Loch na dTrí gCaol.

Dearcán was dementedly curious about de affairs of dis world and would debrief dose who had come in contact wit' de Roman religion ~ a belief system he liked to debunk ~ and ask what dress was worn by dis disconcerting new sect, were dey dapper, were dey dwarfish or dominant in stature, did dey drag deir feet, had dey de power of divination, could dey distil spirits, were dey dirty, deviant, diplomatic or whatever; did dey believe in de Deluge, why do dey go ding-dong, ding-dong, ding-dong; were dey given to debauchery, or dossing; were deir doodles any bigger dan ours; what's a deacon, what's a diocese, what's determinism, what's dualism, and de devil knows what else.

De world is drowning in decadence and decay, he declaimed, wit' disdain. Disease will be rife, disorder will dominate, deception will be de law of all domains. Decimalization is on de cards.

None of de dear denizens of Doire an Draoi had de faintest notion what dis doyen was droning on about but it sounded deep. Beware of de decuman, de tent' wave. Might it be drivel?

Decline and degeneracy have already set in. Soon people will down tools, unable to make decisions for demselves. Decorousness will be a ting of de past. Respect for de old and de decrepit will go out de door. Dedication? Daring? Decency? In deir place defeatism, depression. *Dinnseanchas*, de knowledge of placenames, will disappear. No one will know where de river Dall is. We'll be left wit' de dregs. Defamation, defilement, defenestration... all dese will become dangerously common. Diddering, doodling, dawdling will reach epidemic proportions in all districts. Where nettles grow, no dock leaves will be discovered. Dodgems instead of chariots. Look out for de *damsaire dubh*, de morris-dancer.

Dearcán prophesied many disturbing wonders, divulging by degrees all de secrets dat had lain dormant in his dour heart, a heart he now dredged dramatically, dispensing wisdom so dat his people would not be deluded or duped.

His disciples grew in number, hanging on dearly to every desultory syllable. Much, of course, eluded dese dopey dimwits. Why had Dearcán warned dem about de coming of de dee-jay? What difference will it make to deir lives? What is a dee-jay anyway? How might dey defend demselves? Dibbles were sharpened and dirks dazzled...

Dey milled around him as he dined, as he drawled, as he doodled, as he diddled away de afternoon – damn it, even as he defecated – for none could get enough of our dotty deipnosophist.

Déja vu will be experienced in large doses by delirious dames at child-birt', he deliberated, chewing a diced dumpling. Children will experience dizziness, dehydration, dyslexia, diabetes, slipped discs, dislocations and an un-defined drooping. Young die-hards will have duodenal ulcers, problems wit' de digestive tract and double dementia. Ireland will be denuded of her oak groves. Desecration. Disruption. Dere will be a plague of daddy-long-legs descending from de dome of heaven, or possibly even de devil's coach horse.

Which one, people now dared to ask demselves as rumours drifted dat Dearcán was not devoid of delusions – de effects, no doubt, of de demon drink. Casting deir doubts aside, nonedeless, dey hearkened once more to deir doomsday demagogue, not having de discipline to demolish his one-sided dialogues, decrees and dirges.

Dearcán was a bit of a dentist, too, in his own right, and when he tired of denouncing dis and dat and de od'er, or when hoarse, he would drag out de odd toot' wit' dynamic dexterity or deftly replace a full set of dentures wit' his own duck-feet brand. De dumbfounded denizens of Doire an Draoi drummed up a dolorous din when Dearcán drilled deir defunct molars.

Old customs will die out and de first to depart will be de *deoch an dorais*. Dere will be a Department for dis and a Department for dat – unlike now when de Druid embodies all de knowledge we desire. Depopulation, deportation and drudgery will come about. Distortion. Divilment. Deirdre will go to Scotland. In deir utter depravity, people will eat drisheen and become distended. It depresses me to tink about it, sighed Dearcán. Dark clouds in droves over Ireland, defying description. Dire! De soul of de Celt will be desecrated and his mind will dry out in a dugout in some diminishing desert. And you can forget about de *dán direach*. I despair to dream about it. De red deer will pursue de hound.

His audience daily grew more desperate. Some began to despise him and dropped out, calling him a despot, a *dúramán*.

Our very language is destined for oblivion, he tundered. It will be dross! Dadaism will be devised. A Connaught poet, Daithen, will be demolished by a tree. A man called Saul will ride to Damascus and den he will be Paul. Danes will arrive ~ doubt it not ~ raping and pillaging as dey go. *"Dechrad!"* ~ hardship!

A poet by de name of Dante will go to hell. From Darjeeling will come leaves and we shall be drinking de brew made from dese leaves (yeah, even in dark and dowdy Donegal). We shall be informed by a certain Darwin dat we are monkeys. A Druid called Dev will dream in de Dáil of delightful maidens dancing at crossroads. Dere will be much debate about de national debt. Scrolls will be found by de Dead Sea. A warrior called Delaney will be given gold in a land down under. I see a fighting man and his name shall be Dempsey. I hear a song... diamonds are forever? No, not dat one... Buddy, can you spare a dime... Dat's de one. A flightless bird, de dodo, will disappear. Our music will be not'ing but a diddly-diddly-eye-de-dumb. Tara will be dust and in its place Dublin. Dere will be a crackdown on drunken driving. Dynamite will be invented and a peace prize offered in de inventor's name. Dr Devious will win de Derby. Dastardly tings will be going on in Donnybrook. De Lambeg drum making a deafening din. It will be dog-eat-dog. As to de *dant-mír*, de food we place between de teet' of de dead – demolished. Defunct.

De more he spoke de more it all sounded like Double Dutch.

"Dolenta, dolenta!" – difficult to follow – dey demurred to each od'er.

Far beyond Hy-Brazil, where only de dolphins drift, will be born a man by de unlikely name of Dwight. To de east, a settlement called Dresden in flames. In Dachau, deat', deat', deat'. A Druid-Christian, designated as Colm Cille, will leave Ireland in his boat, de Derg Drúchtach, de red dewy one. Dere will be a duck called Donald and he will make de whole world dribble wit' laughter. De Dalai Lama will go into exile. The *Dandy* will go digital. A distinguished dude will cross de Delaware. Decommissioning will be put on hold. I take little delight in deflating you like dis, Dearcán de Druid declared, but I am determined to let it all out! Homer will return as a Dumbkopf and say, "Doh!"

Dere was no way of stopping him, of detonating Dearcán. He led his followers down many a dusty detour. In time dey were physically and mentally devastated, debilitated, down in de dumps. Yet Dearcán drooled on, developing his depressing diatribe defiantly.

De world is becoming devoid of meaning, he disclosed. Dew will not glisten at dawn or dusk; dairy-maids will not sing deir devotional ditties to de Daghda; it's diabolical. Dialects will be deconstructed. You've heard my diagnosis – drastic. Do I have to draw a diagram? *"Dograing!"* – distress!

Apart from de dee-jay, asked a doting devotee, what od'er dangers lie ahead?

Diapers, came de reply. What de deuce is a diaper? Also, de dildo. De Doberman. De dole. Dialectical materialism.

Détente. De doughnut "Ruaidhrí Ó Dubhghaill!" ~ Roddy
Doyle! Dope. Diaphragms. Detectives. Democracy.
Devolution. Downloading. Debugging... Dallas... It will be
difficult to decipher. Discipline and duty will be defunct.
De Paps of Dana will be destabilized, deir dignity and
dimensions destroyed. Old forms of greetings will go out
de door and deployed instead will be such dreck as "Dia
duit" and "How-dee-do-dee?" (But I digress, he muttered.)
Hoards of sugar-daddies will come and go on de DART,
worried about deposits, dividends, de dollar and de
deutschmark. De dilemma at our doorstep will last until
December of de year 2016. Druidism will den return.
Diligence will be de order of de day. Dilettanti will
emigrate, disgraced, disintegrated. Drum majorettes will
fall over demselves in de dust, as dey deserve. Yes, my
darlings, two tousand years is long enough to be eating
dirt, is it not? *"Dar mo debroth!"* ~ By my doom!

Dey nodded ~ who could disagree?

I, Dearcán de discerning one, disclose dese tings to you.
It is not my desire to discombobulate you or discomfort
you. Let ye not be disconsolate, ye who are discriminating
enough to know de meaning of our discourse.

He ran a dangly, dejected digit t'rough his dull dishev-
elled mop. He looked distracted. Drained. Dismayed. Shall
we discuss dis in greater detail? In terms of deconstruction?
What do ye want, a discount? Direct debit? De donkey will
piss on de floppy disk, he said, swaying. Was he becoming
delirious? Doubloons will be recovered from de duodenum
of de deep. I see devouring dragons, displacement, deat',
and draconian days ahead. De dinner fork? Deplorable.
Do you know what dey're going to call de *Dothra*? Dear
me! De Dodder! De Dodder! *Dord na murduchann,* de
mermaids' chanting, never to be heard again.
"Dofulaing!" ~ Pain dat defies description!

It began to drizzle. Soon de rain was driving down but none dared disperse.

Ireland will be a dump. A drenched, dolmenless dung-heap. Do ye hear – ye droopy dunderheads! Dunces, dim-wits, de whole damn lot of you. Dick-heads!

Slowly de good denizens of Doire an Draoi, drenched to de skin and toroughly disgruntled, reached for deir daggers and silently disembowelled deir druid. Dribbling, dey dined on his dismembered body... *disjecti membra poetae*... delicately dunking his dainties in dusk-hued dill-water. He was delicious.

The silent swish-swish
of Dust Blowers

We were to meet in the bar of the Vidarbha Cricket Club, situated about 15 kilometres from Nagpur, the navel of India. I was over there to write a colour piece for an Irish newspaper. The Irish team were faring well and were due to play another important game in a week's time. My real interest was in poetry, not cricket, however, and Sandeep is a poet. He writes in Marathi which has about 90 million speakers world wide. (I looked it up.) I wanted to talk to him about his 20 years of silence.

As I waited, some youths were dusting the floor, the tables and even the walls of the bar. In a dazed manner. One of them was dusting the door, the door-knob, and even its hinges. These sleep-walking youths were identified on their jackets as Dust Blowers. I hadn't come across this term before. It struck me as very bizarre. No noise they made, no sound at all, swishing away in a soundless universe all of their own.

I was in a silent film. No dust, as far as I could see. Not a speck. They worked away blindly, sometimes exchanging glances, or looking over in my direction. I detected neither hope nor despair in those eyes. Nothing. They swished. Vacantly. It wasn't work. By no stretch of the imagination could you call it work. It was a dance, a slow dance with the rise and fall of invisible dust particles. *Leela.* The sport of the gods.

Initially, I wasn't put out in the least by the furtive glances of the Dust Blowers. I had other things on my mind. I was eagerly looking forward to my meeting with Sandeep. After a while, I have to admit, the Dust Blowers began to get on my nerves. What were they doing all this time? My overactive imagination conjured up images of arcane and malevolent rituals. Any minute now I expected something bizarre to bloom in front of me. My rational self chided me, however, and the fantasy melted away.

Sandeep had a reputation for elusiveness, but he had agreed to meet me because I was Irish. The Irish know how to knock back a peg or two, he said. He knew his whiskey, too, did our Sandeep. He enquired whether I knew that Scotch is "whiskey" without an "e".

Yes, I knew there was a difference although, to to be honest, I wasn't sure which one had the "e". We would be drinking Indian whisky, which wasn't bad at all, he assured me.

Alone and with three waiters at my bidding, I thought I'd get a start on Sandeep and ordered myself a wee dram. It had a preposterous pseudo-Highland name which I will not repeat here (out of respect for my fellow Gaels). I asked for some water. A bottle was produced and, with some cere-mony, shown to me for approval. You would have thought I had ordered some rare and expensive vintage.

The bottle was opened. Before long, a jug appeared and the precious water was ceremoniously poured into the jug. I added some of this by now sacramental water from the jug to the whisky and savoured a sip or two. The three waiters and the Dust Blowers looked on, impassively.

"Quite good" my demeanour seemed to suggest, and all present were relieved. Was I thinking, or behaving, like one of those imperialists of old? Devilishly close, I thought. Watch yourself!

I opened *The Times of India* and read a story about a monkey that was involved in a road accident. It took the Fire Brigade four hours to free the wretched thing. They brought him to the vet and the prognosis was that he would live. I am glad.

I tried to imagine a similar scene back home. How would a Fire Brigade in Athlone, let's say, respond to an emergency like this?

"Is that Pat? Pat, howya, Sergeant O'Brien here, Pat. That's right. Not too bad now. Not too bad at all. Can't complain. Yourself? Good man. Listen, Pat, you probably have better things to be doin' and what with the cutbacks and all but listen here to me, we have this badger here and ~ a badger, that's right, Pat. Needs to be cut out from under a car..."

It would never happen, would it? Not on your life. But the monkey is sacred in India. They have their own monkey-god, Hanuman. Everything is sacred here. There could be a whisky god for all I know.

The Dance of the Dust Blowers was getting under my skin. I stood up and walked to the window. Then something incredible happened. Ordinary enough in a way, and yet... Was it a dream? An illusion? I stood at the window. My gaze ~ fixed on nothing in particular, the blue flowers of the jacaranda ~ my gaze was drawn upwards and filled with the bluest sky I had ever seen.

Just then a dragonfly floated by, and through its bluish translucent wings I saw a blue train chugging merrily along. All thought drained from me in a terrible whoosh. I was nowhere and yet everywhere at the same time. It was all over in a matter of seconds. When I had collected my thoughts again, the first thing I asked myself was, "Is this what the Indians call *moksha*? Freedom? Release? (From what?) Enlightenment?" I laughed at the notion. Whatever it was, it was gone and the blueness of everything was also about to disappear. The day was gone, the dragonfly gone, the train had disappeared.

I returned to my seat, my feet unsteady. I needed to compose myself. No, that was not it. I needed to pinch myself. And I did. I actually pinched myself, not caring whether I was being observed or not. I was wearing a short-sleeved shirt and I examined my arm, where I had pinched myself. How tanned I had become in the space of three days: evenly tanned. The pale circle where once I had worn a wedding band (for thirty-two years) looked ghostly and forlorn. Sweet Jesus, I whispered aloud and the Dust Blowers turned round and stared at me, as one.

The head waiter approaches me, carrying a silver tray. What's this? I haven't ordered the bill. "Message," he says in a sombre voice. A note lies on the silver tray.

The head waiter holds the tray in front of me. I take the note and thank him. I search for my glasses but cannot find them. The head waiter notices that I have left them on the table. "Glasses, sir?" and he hands them to me. It's a message from the poet. "Delayed. All my love, Sandeep." I look at the message a couple of times. I turn it around. Nothing on the back. I re-read it a number of times. All my love? How gushing, from someone I haven't even met yet. Delayed? What does that mean, exactly? Delayed by an hour? A day? A week?

A feeling of unease came over me. I folded the note and placed it in my pocket. My eyes wandered towards the window. No point in standing over there again. Every fibre of my being wanted that moment to re-occur but I knew that it was a once-off. I had caught a glimpse of the Unknown, the unutterable, the unnameable, and that was that. Do with it what you will, a voice seemed to say, but do not ask for it again.

I'm in a glass case, a fish bowl, looking out at the world. Outside, the darkness is falling rapidly. I see a crow open its beak, but no sound emerges. Fireflies are probably congregating in the gardens by now. I long to hear a familiar voice, a familiar accent. I ring home.

Hello? The phone rings and rings. Then I hear my own voice saying that I am out of the country and that I will be back at the end of the month. Then nothing. Only silence. A reflux of cheap whisky sears my throat. How could I possibly have forgotten that she has left me?

The Krushchëv shoe

Randall is one of the leading collectors of antiques and curios in both Ireland and Britain. His name is legend among his peers.

Four or five major American museums are keen to get their hands on some of his more unusual artefacts. He won't part with one iota; no, not even the most seemingly insignificant object. He would rather give his soul away than see his collection pass into a stranger's hands.

The dictates of fashion, or his own feelings, never intrude on Randall's judgement, relying as he does on objective, written reports from trusted agents around the world. Most collectors of his acquaintance and their agents tend to be specialists in their own relatively narrow subject area. Randall's collection is marked by its individuality and diversity.

After all, doesn't he own the magic wand once used by Crowley himself ("the Great Beast"), a treasure he picked up in Iceland, no less! He'd been offered 95,000 dollars for it. He didn't bother to respond to the fax that offered him this princely sum as the fax had been sent to him from a source not known to him. He had his own agents and functionaries in various parts of the world to filter such messages.

Randall was a born collector. No sooner was he snatched from the breast than he began to acquire historical artefacts and various other miscellaneous items. He started by collecting lollipop sticks, match boxes, and toilet rolls in addition to stamps, coins, dead insects, and empty lipstick holders thrown out by his mother, a lady who moved in society.

Later in his career, not only did he collect a great variety of items but he began to note their provenance more carefully, prices paid (when such a history was available), where he had first seen or eventually acquired the item, date of purchase, and sundry other details. Everything was carefully noted down in his thick accounts ledger.

Those in the know claim that this ledger is worth a great deal in itself. All of the annotations were done with scholarly neatness, each nugget of information carefully recorded, and each item's colourful history over the course of several generations carefully described.

Randall was never a vain individual. His morning and afternoon *toilette* consisted mainly of keeping his pencil-thin moustache neat and free from nicotine stains. His annual routine was nearly as regular as his daily ablutions. He kept his own council in controversial matters and dusted down his antique collection once a week. Once a year, on his birthday, he gave himself an illicit treat when he hired an Asian prostitute and paid her to feign an orgasmic frenzy. This year, in perfect symmetry with Randall's age, it was in room number 47 of the Burlington Hotel; no sooner had he finished listening to her cries of pleasure than he immediately booked room 48 for the following year. A man of simple needs.

Fort Knox is what his fellow antique collectors had nicknamed his spacious apartment in Ballsbridge. As implied by this nickname, Randall was also a collector of locks in addition to everything else. He collected door-locks, gate-locks, handcuffs, not to mention a chastity belt he had hanging on the wall. In truth, you'd have to be a

Houdini and a cat burglar combined to gain entry to Randall's pad.

He had a particular hatred of journalists, rumour-mongers, and photographers – those photography masters whose work he collected excepted. No fear that any of those blackguards would ever find out about Khrushchëv's shoe, the shoe that the Soviet leader had removed to use as a hammer on his delegate desk at the UN. This shoe was the sole item in his entire collection the existence of which wasn't noted in his ledger and which wasn't always kept under lock and key. Instead, he carried the shoe with him everywhere he went, hidden deep in the folds of his overcoat. Nobody, not even the snoopiest journalist, would have suspected that he carried it everywhere with him. Who knows? Given an extra tip, the Asian prostitute might permit him to give her a good leathering with it when his next birthday came around? What bliss!

This shoe was the jewel in the crown. As trophies go, it even surpassed the ornate tiger-skin rug from Tibet – a rug the centre of which had already been worn thin by five generations of lamas. It was even better than that enchanting letter written by the author of *The Islandman*, Tomás Ó Criomhthain...

It was two months after the fall of the Soviet bloc that he clinched the deal. He received a fax from Prague and was on the next plane. Soon after landing, he recognized a number of his fellow antique-collectors who had already arrived in this ancient city. A few of them were mooching around in the guise of tourists. He spotted that agent of McGregor's, whatever his name was, and that idiot from Glasgow. Even Kleinstein himself was there, all the way from Pittsburgh. By a strange coincidence, all three of his competitors found themselves in the same pub one day, an Irish bar, the *James Joyce*.

Randall was drinking an Irish coffee, McGregor's agent was on the whiskey and Kleinstein was drinking wine – this in an establishment where most of the customers drank beer and Guinness. Each of the collectors pretending they hadn't noticed any of the others while Randall had his nose stuck in a literary journal called *Trafika*, published by some American ex-pats based in Prague. Despite his best efforts, Randall found himself unable to concentrate on the piece he was reading – an extract from a novel by a Vietnamese writer, translated into English. In fact, it wasn't long before he left the journal down and went back to his hotel.

Huh! Kleinstein! You can be damned sure he'd swipe the journal the minute Randall was gone. Kleinstein, the specialist! A so-called expert in Church furnishings and the man wasn't even a Christian. Kleinstein was Jewish, for God's sake! Maybe that's the reason why his conscience never seemed to bother him as Orthodox treasures from Eastern Europe made their way back to his lair. Kleinstein with his chalices and icons and sanctuary lamps. And the same fellow had probably never even heard of Khrushchëv!

14,000 dollars! Sure, what is 14,000 dollars really when all is said and done? It's nothing when you had a treasure as unique as Nikita Khrushchëv's shoe in your possession. Come the end of the century and this shoe will double in price! Questions of value and price didn't make a whit of difference to Randall one way or another. The Russians had sworn "on the Tsar's bones" that they wouldn't tell a soul, living or dead, who had bought the shoe from them. And Randall had done business with them before, of course.

Sure, there were blackguards and chancers amongst them... but blackguards who wouldn't let you down. The Russian Mafia knew their stuff. They were wise enough to know that it made no sense to fall out with Randall's agents in the antiques game; it would be the kiss of death for them to get into dispute with any *bone fide* antique collector.

Ever since the so-called Hitler Diaries, buyers and sellers were being extra cautious. Having checked and re-checked the available documented evidence, it seemed absolutely certain that this shoe was indeed worn by Khrushchëv himself in New York, 12 October 1960.

In a way that he could not fully articulate, his purchase of the shoe in Prague was the apex of his collecting career. Stations of the Cross, ornate baptismal fonts, an ancient church organ – intact, these were the collectibles which McGregor and Kleinstein chased down, always in the knowledge that theirs was a race against time. Let them – the fools! What business did he have with stained-glass windows and mosaic side-altars? Randall wanted artefacts around him, as furniture to touch and feel in the privacy of his own domain, or objects to carry around unknown to the world, not as treasures to be viewed in museums and galleries.

Even today, nobody knows how Kleinstein managed to transport that fifteenth-century church pulpit all the way back to Pittsburgh. Ah, himself and his treasured oak pulpit. Some day – God willing – it will fall down on top of him!

Occasionally, Randall released Khrushchëv's shoe from its dark haven in the depths of his coat, showing it to the light, polishing it gently. He would set the shoe down in front of him and worship it in all its hidden glory. This was a shoe that millions had seen when it pounded the desk and seen by countless millions since in photographs. In these private moments, he would smell the shoe, inhaling its leathery secret.

Two years later, Randall goes to answer a caller at the front door of his apartment. He has already checked the security monitor. The postman is there with a registered parcel for him. The parcel is postmarked Pittsburgh. On opening it, he discovers a video and a note signed in Kleinstein's handwriting. "I hope the shoe isn't pinching..."

The bastard. How the hell did Kleinstein ~ who told him ~ what the hell?

Randall puts the video in the recorder and presses "Play". A slight trickle of perspiration falls from the tip of his thin moustache. The film is in black and white. It shows Khrushchëv beating the desk with his shoe. The piece of film has a voice-over. Kleinstein, no less, the original soundtrack deleted.

"Oh, that's Khrushchëv's shoe you have, all right, Randall..." In the background he hears Kleinstein in fits of laughter. He is practically choking with mirth.

"But it's not the shoe he struck the table with! Hah! Not at all. Your shoe belongs to the other foot, you fool!"

Kleinstein explodes with laughter again. Randall turns up the sound.

~ Translated from the Irish by Micheál Ó hAodha

Postscript: "Hammarskjöld, shy rather than cold, showed me photographs of Khrushchëv beating his shoe on his desk during that famous incident in the General Assembly. If you looked carefully, you could see that he was wearing both his shoes, which meant that he either borrowed the shoe from a hapless aide, or else that he smuggled the shoe in to the General Assembly in a paper bag, disguised as a sandwich..."

~ Peter Ustinov, *Dear Me*

Hermit

No one ever knew who he really was, or if he had a name. There was no point in asking him either; he couldn't tell you who he was or how he had come to be there. He had taken a vow of silence apparently. He certainly wasn't dumb. The first local to see him overheard him reciting the Rosary, or so he said – "in Irish or some other strange language."

The Hermit lived in a cave near Loch Gur in County Limerick. According to the locals, he did not eat or drink anything, just whatever people left in his food bowl. And although no one ever heard him utter even a syllable that made any sense, there seemed to be an amazing communication between the hermit and his followers. A language simply of eye, eyebrows, and gesture.

Rumour had it that he never slept a wink. His eyes were dark, unruffled pools. Winter and summer, morning and night, he was there before you in the mouth of the cave, sitting silently on a cold bare flagstone. He didn't wear clothes, just a loincloth of sorts covering his genitals, a cloth made out of bird skin. An old hag would arrive from County Clare once a month to wash his loin-cloth and to clean out the cave – or so it was said anyway.

People claimed that he was a Christian but it was impossible to tell. In the course of time, an American professor named Simon Woods arrived to investigate the case. He had the locals tormented. Afterwards, he wrote an article based on his findings. Very nasty in tone, to put it mildly. He was highly critical of the local people, considering them to be nothing more than a bunch of innocent bumpkins. He referred to the hermit as an Aghori, a word nobody had ever heard of, and his article created quite a rumpus.

The hermit's followers were particularly hurt by the professor's findings. The article was insulting in the extreme, a complete fiction, the sole purpose of which was to offend everyone, the hermit's followers claimed. They managed to get their hands on a few copies of the journal and ceremoniously burned them.

The hermit was originally from India, Professor Woods claimed. He had travelled west to Ireland and all the indications were that he belonged to that esoteric, secretive sect known as the Aghori. The hermit's food-bowl was shaped like a skull. The professor claimed that there was more to this skull-like object than first met the eye; not only was the bowl in the shape of a skull; it actually was a human skull which had been shaped and hollowed out in the form of a food-bowl. The Aghori are a Tantric sect, the professor explained, a group for whom necrophagia is a central aspect of their training and their disgusting rituals.

Woods claimed to have discovered a collection of burnt bones behind the hermit's cave: the Aghori would smear himself with the ashes of these bones; the professor was wholly satisfied that these cinders were indeed the detritus of burned human bones!

Prove it, said the hermit's followers. If you're so sure of your theory, professor, then you have a duty to report this and let the Gardaí call in the State Pathologist. Some of the followers considered him to be the reincarnation of Gearóid Iarla, the Norman-Gaelic earl and necromancer, while others considered him to be the reincarnation of an eternal druid who had lived centuries earlier.

If somebody's cat, hen, or dog went missing, there was a handful of people who blamed the ascetic in the cave; prior to his appearance in the area they would have blamed the fox. Some people were very frightened of him and kept their distance; others remained loyal, no matter what happened.

His followers were said to number around 1,170 although the *Limerick Leader* put the number at much less than this – claiming he only had about eighty followers, at most, at any one particular time. They speculated that many of his early followers had already abandoned him and that the hermit was just another one of those one-week wonders.

"Indeed, it is likely that there are just twenty followers in the core group and the bulk of these are New Age Travellers from England," the newspaper reported. A television crew came over to make a documentary about the hermit at one stage but they left again within three days. A spokesperson said: "Not only would the hermit not speak to us – his followers refused to be interviewed. It's impossible to attempt a half-hour documentary on some dumb character who simply sits on a flagstone, never uttering a word."

The documentary-maker had miscalculated however. Had he waited another week or two, he would have seen some action. He just didn't have the patience for it.

Local opinion was divided. What had drawn his followers to him in the first place? Simple curiosity? Devotion? Superstition and mumbo-jumbo? One person maintained that the hermit drew people to him with his eyes. His eyes emitted a strange glow, or so the man claimed. There was a peculiar radiance in his eyes, as though he were staring into all the stars of the firmament.

"Nobody has ever seen him blink," another claimed.

"He never closes his eyes..."

"An old crone visits him occasionally to shave him!"

"He never laughs..."

"Is this creature human at all? Does he ever go for a piss, say?"

"Stop! Don't talk like that about him! Have a bit of respect for God's sake! The man is a living saint!"

"A saint, is it?"

"I'm telling you. A born saint. Didn't he rid me of the gout!"

The hermit carried a big stick. A fine blackthorn stick. His followers referred to this cudgel as "the holy crozier". The hermit would scrawl strange patterns, mysterious esoteric messages, with the crozier on the ground, then wipe them away again before anybody had a chance to interpret them.

One of the New Age Travellers from England, a young woman of about thirty years of age, said that she saw some of these scrawls in the shape of snakes and other serpents, and a few of them crawled away from the spot. Nobody took much notice of this woman, however, as she regularly took drugs and people assumed that she was having hallucinations.

Occasionally, the hermit would draw a big circle on the ground. These circles of his were so exact that a mathematics teacher from Tralee said that they were better than anything people could draw with the aid of a compass. People were astounded by this piece of information.

One day the hermit's followers brought him a woman who was suffering from madness. The woman's hair was tied up in a big bunch on the back of her head and what did the hermit do first but ask her to release it and let it hang free. He stared at the woman intently for a period of about twenty minutes as a crowd looked on. Then, without any warning, the hermit called out in strange wonderful tones. His words sounded something like this:

CLING TRING CRING AH-HOOM

Once he'd said this, the woman convulsed. She had some kind of a fit. Her tongue swelled in her mouth and her limbs shook uncontrollably. She went deathly pale and when she grabbed hold of her own throat, the people thought that she was going to choke. She began to laugh instead ~ and in a loud manly voice to boot!

Jay jay jay ~ jay Kāli Mā! the woman chanted and the hermit raised three of his fingers into the air, a gesture which one person interpreted as a reference to the Holy Trinity ~ God the Father, the Son, and the Holy Spirit. It was a sign of God's blessing, some said, while others interpreted the gesture in a different light. The woman was possessed by three demons which the hermit was attempting to drive out.

He drew a circle in the mud with his blackthorn. Then he placed his hand on the afflicted woman's head, the very crown, and made a gesture as if to remove a louse which he then placed in the circle. This action was repeated in respect of her neck and stomach.

"He has done the *ciorradh-má-gcuach* on those demons now, mangled them like you would mangle a flea between your thumbnails," one of the hermit's followers whispered excitedly under his breath. No sooner had these words been uttered, but the hermit pointed to the follower who had thus whispered and indicated that he should empty out his pockets.

The man produced a knife, a packet of cigarettes, matches, a naggin of whiskey, a wallet, and a biro. The only items that the hermit evinced any interest in however were the whiskey, the wallet and the matches.

He opened the wallet and removed a twenty-euro note, a tenner, and a fiver. He placed the money in the circle and proceeded to burn it. Far from being upset at the hermit's action, his follower was thrilled to be chosen as the person who would assist his master in this ceremony.

The hermit swallowed whatever bit of whiskey was left in the naggin and spat the alcohol onto the flames. Merciful God! If you only heard the eerie cry that came out of the flames. It would have put the heart crossways in you for a month. Down in the Glen, the people said that it must have been the sound of a Banshee Convention with all of them crying in unison.

The mad woman was immediately healed of her affliction. Nothing, human or demonic, ever afflicted her again. Shortly after this incident, the Bishop of Limerick issued an instruction to his flock warning them against frequenting the hermit or having any involvement in his pagan rituals. The Church was satisfied with Professor Woods's assessment of the situation. The hermit, or the man known as "the stranger", was an Aghori and his peculiar powers came from darkness and not from light.

In Newcastle West, in Kilfinane, and in Bruree a couple of people walked out of their local church in defiance of this on the Sunday that the announcement was made. The Bishop was shocked when he heard this and he sought advice on the matter from other senior ecclesiastics. He even met with the Papal Nuncio, a man by the name of Monsignor Nadiani. Monsignor Nadiani said that he would have word about this issue with a friend of his who was a T.D. – a representative in the Irish parliament.

The local pharmacists and doctors weren't too fond of the hermit either as he seemed to have cured a number of people from illnesses that appeared terminal. There was talk of miracles occurring and the numbers going on diocese pilgrimage to places such as Lourdes and Fatima fell by 28%.

The controversy dragged on for a while, until, in the end, a Fianna Fáil T.D. came up with a master-plan (as designed by Nadiani) to resolve the crisis. In between times, the *Irish Times* published a letter from somebody who questioned Professor Woods's academic credentials. This person also alleged that the professor's researches on the hermit were actually being funded by a leading preacher from the Bible Belt in the southern United States. This was one of those preachers who hated any religion other than the one he had set up himself – a church that went by the name of "The Temple of Jesus Christ, Son of the Most High".

The next day saw the Professor interviewed in the same newspaper where he denied any link to the TJCSMH or any other church for that matter. In addition to this he stated: "I am quite familiar with this Indian charlatan and his tricks. I have been after him for a full fifteen years at this stage, pursued him all over the world: no matter where he goes, the fiend keeps evading me somehow. He's as slippery as an eel. My research notes indicate that the charlatan is following the instructions of his own guru, a man who has ordered him to travel throughout the world, setting up shrines to Kāli, the goddess of destruction, wherever he goes. This isn't scare-mongering! I came across him in both Mexico and Peru! I even followed him as far as Madagascar. This guy knows damn well that I am writing a book about him. All will be revealed in the book! He knows this and he is putting every barrier that he can think of in my way. I suffered an awful bout of diarrhoea in Tokyo while a crowd of monkeys attacked me in Gibraltar – each of these incidents was arranged by the Aghori, I'm sure of it. In Indonesia, he was thrown into prison for not having a visa and what did the son of a bitch do? He magicked a visa out of nowhere. I have solemn proof that this happened, proof provided under oath by one of the Prison Officers there, a man who has since been promoted to the position of Assistant Governor of that same prison. The Aghori shut his fist tight and when he opened it again there was a spanking new passport in his hand, a fully authorized and stamped visa. Would you believe it? They had no option but to set him free again..."

Bernie Condon, the local T.D. for the part of Limerick that the hermit was then operating in, officially designated the area a nature reserve, a story that made the front page of the *Limerick Leader*. Nobody would be permitted entry to this area ever again without permission from the regional Board of Works.

Local environmentalists supported Condon's decision, citing the diversity of rare mushrooms and flowers found in the area as good enough reason for this ban. Not only was the area where the hermit operated environmentally unique, Lough Gur, one of the earliest and most important historical sites in Europe, was just down the road. The last corncrake in Ireland was heard singing in those fields, a bird that "I heard with my own ears," Condon said.

Monsignor Nadiani phoned the T.D.

"Condon? May God forgive you. The last corncrake in Ireland? Give me a break..."

The two men burst out laughing. The hermit's followers argued that there was no point in designating the area a nature sanctuary if nobody could ever visit it but their pleas fell on deaf ears. They had lost the battle before it had even begun. They would have to persuade the hermit to leave the cave somehow – to kidnap him if needs be –

he would die of starvation if they didn't get him out of there as nobody could get to him and fill his food-bowl any more.

That Sunday morning five of them made for the cave. They were debating amongst themselves. Would the hermit leave willingly? Would he settle down happily in a house the same as anybody else? What experience had he of a bed, a hot water bottle, central heating, or television? Would civilization kill him?

They heard a curlew cry out in the sky. The morning was beautiful, full of sun showers. They found themselves silently agreeing with Condon's view of the place. It was truly a nature sanctuary. The vegetation was lush and the fields and woods were thick with beautiful flowers.

Approaching the cave, they came to a sudden stop. There was no sign of the hermit in his usual spot at the mouth of the cave. He had disappeared. They broke into a run:

"Hello, hi. Hey ~ anyone at home?" They searched the cave inside and out. The strangest thing of all was that they could see the tracks their own feet had made in the mud and yet there was no sign anywhere of the hermit. As if he had never been there. All that was left of him was a circle in the gravel, the traces of which were already on the point of disappearing in the mist.

~ Translated from the Irish by Mícheál Ó hAodha

King of the Jungle

Jason failed every single subject in the Junior Certificate exam. He didn't do much better in the Leaving Certificate either. He got one pass grade – in History. That was it. His mother was very worried on the day the results were issued. She was afraid in case Jason decided to do anything stupid that he might later regret. Her real fear was that he might harm himself in some way or – God forbid – that he would be struck down with depression again.

What would she do if that were to happen? Where would she find anybody else to help her? Since she had been widowed, she had retreated into herself and had very little contact with either relatives or friends. Jason was the centre of her life since the death of her husband. She was really worried about Jason, the flesh of her flesh. What if he never found a niche of his own, something that would make him happy and content? What if he turned out like his father?

"You needn't worry about me, Ma," was Jason's mantra. His mother imagined the worst, however. She saw him falling by the wayside. She was afraid a life of insecurity lay ahead of him, that the frustrations of a young man would lead to his falling in with the wrong company and God knows what else, frittering his life away on gambling, dole, and drink.

Jason wasn't too worried about his Leaving Cert results. "Getting all these points, it's not exactly the be-all and the end-all is it?"

"You're not too disappointed about the results, so?"

"Disappointed? Not at all. I wasn't expecting anything much anyway. That pass in History was a bonus," he said, grinning.

She prayed to Padre Pio for Jason and over time she was convinced that her prayers were answered. Her worries about him gradually receded. Jason was happy in himself, or so it seemed anyway. He was healthy and was hanging around with a nice crowd. A young man in his prime, just twenty years a-growing.

"God is strong and He has a good Mother..."

The anxieties she had felt about him in his teenage years had dissipated. In their place was a new-found serenity and even a sense of pride.

Jason was minding himself very well. He was always neat and tidy in appearance now and looked content. He did more than his fair share of work around the house. Ironing and all the rest of it. He was a great lad, really. She never had need of a plumber or electrician. He was handy and fixed everything himself. It might take him a day or two sometimes to complete a job if it was a complicated one, but he got to the bottom of every problem in the end. If he had to go to the library and consult some manual or other, it was no bother to him. He would do whatever was necessary so that the job was done properly and to his satisfaction.

If the doors were squeaking, he oiled them while whistling contentedly to himself. It was the same with every other part of the house. He fixed window frames and taps, cleaned out drains and pipes. Whatever needed doing, he saw to it. He was always energetic, had great patience, no matter how long-drawn-out or boring the task in question. Wasn't it a wonder that he had done so badly at school? Maybe he was one of those lads who never received any encouragement from his teachers, his mother thought. Hadn't one of the teachers referred to him as an "ape" at one point? But that was a long time ago now. Now he was flying it and nothing seemed impossible when he put his mind to it.

"Ah, leave that to me, you ould wan, you!" he'd admonish her when there was hoovering to be done or dishes to be washed. "You sit down there and have a nice rest. Pull in closer to the fire and stretch out for yourself. Would you like to give that crossword another go? I'll run out and get your glasses for you. Where did you leave them last? Ah, here they are. Now... four down, six letters – Alaska, isn't it?

"You're got me spoilt," she'd say and then (under her breath, to herself) "It wasn't from his father's side that he got these fine traits of character."

Once Jason had completed most of the DIY jobs that needed doing around the house, he set to developing something else entirely – himself. Books started coming into the house. She couldn't believe it.

Then one night she got up out of bed and went downstairs as she had heard him below in the kitchen jabbering to himself in some strange language or other! She poked her head in the door and saw Jason staring at a picture of a naked man on the table. It was a picture of the human form as though torn from an anatomy book. Jason was staring intently at this picture while uttering the following:
Rectus femoris
Vastus medialis
Trapezius
Sternocleidomastoid
Omohyoid...

"O Padre Pio," she prayed before returning to sleep that night, "what on earth is happening? Please help me understand. Has he decided to study medicine, despite only achieving one pass grade, in Leaving Cert history?"

She noticed the cans the following afternoon. Her curiosity got the better of her and she opened one of them and sniffed its contents. Inside was a red powder; it was some kind of powdered nutrient supplement.

From then on Jason's eating habits changed. Sometimes he had nothing other than a mixture made of one raw egg, orange juice, and honey for breakfast. His main food seemed to come from these tins of various descriptions – powder that he assured her contained all the minerals, vitamins and proteins that he needed. There were enough nutrients and supplements in these tins to sustain an elephant by all accounts. Every Sunday, Jason ate a big steak. Next he began work on the local neighbourhood, mowing the grass in the parks, cleaning paths and roads of weeds and every other detritus. He began to do odd-jobs here and there, and it wasn't long before there was great demand for his services. He always worked hard and completed every job with absolute efficiency and care, and before long he opened a savings account for himself in the local bank. He was saving up for his future, he said – that and the tins of nutrients that cost a fair whack. This new obsession of his was an expensive one, but wasn't it better than wasting all his money on some flighty girl that wouldn't appreciate it? So his mother thought, anyway.

"You don't mind if I rearrange the garage a bit?" Jason asked one day.

"Not at all, love. That would be great! What use has that place been to us since your poor Dad died? God rest his soul. Especially seeing as neither of us owns a car or can drive one. What are you thinking of doing with the garage anyway, if you don't mind me asking?"

"I was thinking of making it into a small gym for myself! I'll see you later this afternoon! Have to run now as I have a few jobs lined up for today. I have to fix a glasshouse out in Glenageary and cut some hedges out in Rathfarnham!" He gave his mother a quick peck on the cheek and left the house, his old denim jacket thrown over one of his shoulders.

"Don't be killing yourself working now, my little angel," his mother called after him as he jogged up the road. A few seconds later, she wondered why she had referred to him as a little angel. It wasn't a term that suited him really. No, he wasn't a little angel anymore. Far from it; he was now a fine big block of a man, God bless him. And yet it was strange that he had never received any Valentine's cards. Not even once! Still, it was good to see him so busy!

When Jason was gone, his mother went out to the garage to see what old rubbish she could clear out before Jason got down to work. The next three weeks were a whirl of activity as Jason set about his latest project with a feverish energy. He worked late into the night, hammering concrete and nailing wood, sawing and drilling. He made a hell of a racket, so much so that some of the neighbours began enquiring when this late-night project of his was likely to be completed.

Once he had the toughest jobs out of the way, Jason focused in on the finer points of his project – he began cleaning the garage and polishing the wood; he painted and decorated everything that needed to be done. Finally, the big day arrived and his mother invited the woman who lived next door for the official unveiling of Jason's gym. They had tea and biscuits and headed out for the "official" unveiling. The neighbour was blown away by Jason's handiwork. He had done a really beautiful job on what had been a mouldy filthy garage for years.

"Any chance that you could move in with me for six months?" the woman next door said to Jason, winking cheekily at him all the while. The new mini-gym was an incredible sight with its assortment of weights set out on polished timberwork and all the sophisticated frames and balancing bars. Its floor was scoured clean. It was absolutely spotless, so clean that you could have eaten your dinner off it.

"Mark my words ~ what he's done to that old garage has added another €5000 to the price of this house," the neighbour remarked to Jason's mother.

"It must have, all right. Maybe even twice that," the mother replied.

Within the space of six months Jason had installed every single item that a modern sophisticated mini-gym could boast. Some of these exercise and weight machines he had bought for cash; others he had bought in accordance with a pre-agreed instalment option.

His mother couldn't see the point of the exercise bike.

"Would you not get yourself a real bike and head out into the fresh air of the Wicklow mountains? What's the point of having a bicycle inside in a garage? It's an unnatural yoke ~ doesn't even have wheels!"

"Ma, I've an entire regime laid out for myself now. The exercise bike is an indispensable part of the regime, every aspect of which needs to be followed to the letter. This is the most modern and state-of-the-art gym anywhere in the country. And, before much longer, I'll have paid everything off too ~ all the fitments and machine."

And when it was all paid for, from that day on Jason never left his new quarters. He was no longer interested in outdoor work such as cutting lawns or helping to clean the

park. He wouldn't even go down the road to the grocery shop to buy his mother some provisions. He didn't have time. He was too devoted to intense exercise and weights-training. He was lord and master of his exercise emporium and the dumbbells, punch-bags, weights and exercise machines were the slaves of his domain.

He spent five hours a day in there now, exercising non-stop. He'd break for a shower then before noting down his progress in a notebook he entitled "Physical Conditioning Diary". He cleaned all of his exercise gear obsessively. Everything was kept in an absolutely immaculate condition; even a speck of grass on his sneakers was enough to get him scrubbing and cleaning fastidiously again. Once the gear was taken care of, he would go into the kitchen to help his mother with the main meal of the day. These days, his mother nagged him to eat more regular food but he said that he had more than enough nutrients in the tins. The evidence was there. He was as strong as an ox with muscles bulging out all over the place.

Occasionally, he liked to try out new and unusual foods and to see what effect they had on his physical conditioning, a mushroom known as "shitake", a type of pickled plum called "umeboshi", various different types of seaweed...

They rarely disagreed about anything. The only thing they ever had any differences about was the occasional night when his mother wanted to watch one of those old films – the likes of *From Here to Eternity* – and Jason preferred to watch sports. In these instances, they generally tossed a coin to decide. Strangely enough, Jason always won these toss-ups although – to give him his due – he generally gave in to his mother when she wanted to watch her favourite actors.

One evening she had an idea and went straight to the gym and said to Jason: "Did it ever occur to you, my angel ~" (and she corrected herself immediately) "~ did you ever think that you might be able to make a living out of this gym business?"

"How do you mean?" asked Jason, frowning.

"What about making the gym available to others on a commercial basis ~ you could be their trainer!"

"Hold on a minute now ~ this is *my* gym."

There was a strange passion in his voice and he became more emotional.

"I built that gym with my own two hands..."

"You did, love, God bless you! I understand that completely. All I'm saying is that ~"

"Anyway, there is room here for only one boss. *Comprende?*"

"Jason!" Her face paled. "Of course... I was only just..."

She turned her back to him. Her heart was pounding. She fished in her pocket for a handkerchief to wipe her eyes.

She got a right fright the next moment when she felt Jason's hand on her shoulder. She spun around quickly.

"J~Jason!" Her eyes were wide with horror. He was standing so close to her that she felt his hot breath on her face. The lenses of her glasses clouded over but as she reached again for her handkerchief, Jason leaped onto the wooden horse that stood in the centre of his gym. He straddled the wooden horse and hunkered down. He looked like a gorilla.

"I'm the King of the Jungle", he hollered, "and there'll be no rotten little monkeys hopping around on my patch."

~ Translated from the Irish by Mícheál Ó hAodha

Lost in Translation

He was constantly urging me to take one of his books away with me. "Any book at all, it doesn't matter, take your choice, whatever grabs your fancy."

Eventually, I became reluctant to call on him since I knew that he'd pressure me to borrow this book or that from him. It did occur to me once or twice that I would have been better off had I just accepted his offer, if only to satisfy him. But why bother with a book that wouldn't be of the slightest interest to me? Would I get further than the cover? If I were to bother to take even one of them, well, Rick would assume that he had me converted. Next thing he'd pursue me hot-foot into whatever pub I drank in, his eyes bright with missionary zeal. Or else, he would start phoning me at home.

"So now... what do you think! Do you still think it's all a load of horse manure, eh?"

Or he'd leave a message with my wife, something along the lines of: "Aha, now he really understands!"

Whatever it was that put me off about his pet subject I never managed more than a quick glance at any of the books he gave me, just the illustrations to be honest. Rick's notes in pencil on the margins of the text I found far more interesting. Even with them, however, my innate cynicism would get the upper-hand on me and I'd leave the book aside almost as quickly as I had picked it up.

I'm fussy about what I read and recently my focus has been on poetry written in French:

Une odeur de tombeau dans les ténebres nage,
Et mon pied peureux froisse, au bord du marécage,
Des crapauds imprévus et des froids limaçons.

We were all square. Rick refused to be swayed by my opinions especially when it came to poetry and when he began reading a few of his favourite pieces aloud ~ albeit uninvited ~ (I would usually mutter "God give me patience" under my breath) ~ I had to switch off and focus on something else. I would close my eyes in order to give the impression that I was concentrating intently on what he was saying. I did this out of politeness. It doesn't cost anything to be polite.

If he stopped momentarily at any point ~ to check that I was listening ~ I would utter a quiet phrase of encouragement ~ something along the lines of "How very mysterious!" or "Who would believe it..." The reverence he showed for this prose ~ if one could call it such ~ was incredible. One could be forgiven for thinking that he was relaying the words of one of the English language's most exceptional stylists, Pater or Ruskin, say.

Rick had only one genre in his collection, probably the most comprehensive of its kind in Ireland. He was a specialist. I had noticed over the years that he was very selective about who might be offered a glimpse of these riches. What is it about me, I wonder, that I manage to draw the likes of Rick on myself? The Honorary Secretary of the Lame-Duck Society is what my wife calls me any time I leave the house with "Have to meet Rick" as an excuse.

And when I'd reach the place where I was supposed to meet him, usually a pub, as often as not no Rick. Lost in one of those books of his, his mind far away. I would sit there alone reading Rimbaud to myself:

Un chant mystérieux tombe des astres d'or.

I met him accidentally on the train one day and he didn't recognize me. I was sitting directly across from him! He was carefully examining a diagram in one of his books ~ upside-down ~ the book was upside-down that is! And if Rick himself had been upside-down, it wouldn't have surprised me unduly either.

"Rick?" I said.

He looked at me ~ or through me ~ to be more exact. He must have been on some other planet.

"Dún Laoghaire! We're here..."

"Oh," he said, looking out the window.

And "Oh" again when he recognized me properly.

He's a strange one. Amongst all of the eccentrics I know, he stands out a mile. I can read the strangeness in his face. In his left eye I see someone who is suffering; in the other eye all I see is a peculiar emptiness, a vacuity beyond explanation.

Rick himself believes that the characteristics of your father can be read in one of your eyes and your mother's in the other. I can't remember now which eye is which or where he discovered this theory.

His favourite pastime is to rise with the lark and head out to the Curragh in Kildare where he gathers magic mushrooms. He places them in a satchel full of his notes and papers so that he could easily pass for a bank official or insurance agent. When he gets home he sorts them and prepares them for a time when he feels the urge to go a bit crazy ~ crazier than he normally is.

So I've heard. I have no actual proof of this of course seeing as he's never once offered to cook me a regular meal ~ never mind a dish of magic mushrooms. My sources tell me that it wouldn't knock a feather out of him to lash back

sixty or more of those magic mushrooms in one sitting. They taste so bland that he bakes them in the oven before-hand and honey-coats them to make them more edible. Wouldn't surprise me.

This time last year I was wandering around a bookshop in Dún Laoghaire looking for a second-hand Verlaine when in walked Rick. He had the look of somebody who had already been in earlier in the day and was now returning to see whether they had found the book that he was looking for. Not the case at all.

"Here. I'll stand you a pint," he said to me. He had a tidy sum in his hand, over a hundred euros. What was on the floor but five boxes of books, from Rick's collection.

"You're not after selling your library Rick, are you?" I said in a horrified whisper, drawing him aside. Actually, it was a whisper mixed with horror and relief, horror that he might have sold his collection, and relief that he might finally have rid himself of his obsession. He gave me a wink.

"What's up? No longer believe in ~?"

Which was more shocking ~ the Pope declaring that God does not exist or Rick getting rid of his precious collection?

"Let's go," he said, grabbing me by the arm. We headed for Dunphy's, Rick walked out into the traffic, weaving between cars and buses as if they weren't even there. He was leading the way like a prophet walking towards the Promised Land.

"You weren't made for this world," I said to myself, as he came to a sudden stop at the door, bowed and ushered me into the pub ahead of him.

I was dying for a pint, although I rarely touch a drop before five o'clock in the evening.

"It's not that I don't believe in the collection anymore," he replied, after I questioned him about it again. "On the contrary. I want to spread the word. I was keeping it to myself for far too long."

"Absolutely. It was about time for you. Haven't you read and re-read everything that has ever been written on the subject!" I said.

His face lit up in a smile.

"Reading is nothing ~ no more than a wren's fart ~ compared to the essence of the thing, the project itself!"

"What thing?"

My heart sank.

He sipped his pint. For the first time since I had known him, I noticed an unusual vitality in the eye that had previously been dulled and dead.

"It happened..."

"What happened?"

"Contact..."

"You're not saying that ~"

"As sure as there's a collar on that pint of yours."

I made a point of not being at home whenever Rick called to the door and after a few weeks he gave up. I began to drink in pubs around Blackrock instead of Dún Laoghaire. I'd hear a rumour about Rick from time to time. That he had become even more odd in his ways, that he sat in the front window of his house staring into space, naked except for a pair of drawers. That he had grown a beard, never ventured out anymore. That he ordered Chinese meals that were delivered to his door ~ noodles, gone completely cracked on noodles. Other rumours did the rounds ~ he had become serious about his writing. The first chapter of his novel had been rejected by publishers in both Ireland and Britain but a company in California had already given him an advance and a deadline of six months in which to complete it. I don't know whether there was substance to any of these rumours. I never did find out.

"I'm delighted that you don't see him anymore," my wife said to me one morning. I didn't react one way or another to this. I know that she thought it was in my best interest to avoid Rick's company; and yet I found myself leaving the house shortly afterwards and taking the train out to Dún Laoghaire. To see Rick. One way or another, I would see for myself how Rick was doing.

I'll never forget that morning as long as I'll live. It was autumn. Overgrown rowan trees crowded his tiny garden, the wan September sun shone hesitantly on the berries that clung to the highest branches.

I came to his house and stood still. I looked up at the branches dotted with berries and they appeared to be strung together as a translucent Rosary, the beads being told by the morning breeze. I tried to compose a line of poetry in French there and then, a metaphor that would encompass the image I had imagined. Than reality intervened and I remembered why I had really come to this house.

Doorbell number three. The doorbell was without a name. His name had been written there previously, hadn't it? I pressed the bell. No response. I pressed it again and again. I waited two or three minutes and then tried it once more ~ just in case he had risen from his bed and was getting dressed before answering the door. No sound came from within. Nothing. I was turning to leave but decided to give it one last go. I tried a different doorbell this time, the bell to flat number two. Next thing, a clattering sound came from within. A young fella in his twenties appeared at the door. He stank of lager.

"Scut," he said to the cat, aiming a kick in her direction.

I apologized for disturbing him and told him that I was looking for a friend of mine from number three, a man by the name of Rick.

"Ricky, is it?"

"Yeah. Rick ~"

"Left a while ago."

"Where did he move?"

"God knows. Went out foreign, I think. Somewhere far away, I hear. Poor Ricky, he was always way out there."

He burst out laughing and drawing a hand across his nose, he slammed the door in my face.

I never keened poor Rick properly. I leave that job to the experts in their trade, the poets:

O douleur! O douleur! Le temps mange la vie ...

I do think of Rick every now and again, however, especially if I notice someone on the bus or on the train reading one of his books. One of the many hundreds of books that he carefully collected and stored before scattering them randomly. The pencil notations on the margins of each tome, every damn one of those books dealing with some aspect of that mad great dream of his, the same bizarre obsession that exercised his daily existence: contact with creatures from other worlds.

~ Translated from the Irish by Mícheál Ó hAodha

What else would the son of a cat do?

...only kill a mouse!

Of course!

I have been a member of *Gaels Anonymous* for fourteen years now, I'd say. Maybe longer, even? You'd think I'd remember considering how fateful a day it was ~ the day I joined up. I was the first to register with an organization which now numbers in the region of 8,ooo members. If it wasn't for *Gaels Anonymous* I'd have gone round the bend by now. Loopy. I'd be like Sweeney, sitting there high up in the branches, deafened by song-birds. Feathers growing out of my rear. *Gaels Anonymous.* If such an organization didn't exist, somebody would have to create it.

Whatever people say and they can say what they like, you can't deny this much ~ there would be no such thing as *Gaels Anonymous* without me. I don't say this out of pride, it's a simple fact. Wasn't it on myself that they did the first tests which proved scientifically that such an addiction existed in the first place, as complex an addiction as any other?

Everybody knows the great work that *Alcoholics Anonymous* does. Society would be in a far more desperate state if it wasn't for *AA*. There would be people left homeless. Poor unfortunates lying by the side of the road, traces of nettle juice on their lips. As true as God.

Funnily enough, it was at a meeting of *Alcoholics Anonymous* that I first heard tell of the concept that is the *Gaels Anonymous* we know today. To be honest, I didn't think that such a group would ever see the light of day, never mind myself having a central role in its foundation. An anonymous alcoholic thinking aloud during therapy and he comes up with this?

Gaels Anonymous is what I need, says he. "Yeah," says I immediately. You've got it spot on there, friend. "*Gaels Anonymous!*" I cried out. Exactly what we need. Previous to this I had got great help with a range of additions – alcoholism, sex addiction, chocolate addiction, gambling addiction, cocaine addiction, and all the rest. (I was even addicted to Facebook at one stage.) I knew deep down that I would never really be healed of any of these cravings if I didn't deal with the biggest addiction of them all. My addiction to the Irish language. I couldn't get enough of this ancient tongue; it was a compulsive craving. I loved it more than the child who loves the breast milk of white-palmed women – as the Scottish poet Ian Lom once put it. In mellifluous Gaelic, needless to say. I loved it more than nectar of the gods – if such a drink exists – as I'm sure it does.

"Hello, I'm Tadhg," announced Tadhg, who was no more a Tadhg than the man in the moon. This man was from Donegal and there wasn't a Donegal man born yet whose name was Tadhg.

"Howya, Tadhg," everybody in the group said back to him, in unison.

"I'm Hiúdaí," announced a Corkman with an educated tone of voice. We all laughed. Wasn't it strange too – the people gathered for that first meeting of *Gaels Anonymous* were an exceptionally clever bunch. In fact, two were brilliant academics.

Irish-language names were permitted in the clinic for purpose of introducing ourselves but after that, the use of Irish was banned. Not a syllable could be uttered; its use was subject to penalties and prohibited at all times. We might as well have been back again in the days of the Tally Stick, an era in which the language was completely out-lawed; that's how repressive they were about it.

This made sense, of course. To continue spouting Irish to each other was similar, say, to a group of alcoholics heading for the *Stag's Head* in order to sample twenty different brands of whiskey as part of a market research exercise. I even heard afterwards that they had banned the Irish name *Tadhg*. "Hello, I'm Timothy." Unbelievable. But there you are. They were afraid that the utterance of even one Irish word ~ a forename like Colmán, Sorcha, or Luisne ~ would exacerbate our withdrawal symptoms and send us over the edge.

Things went on like this for a while. Time passed. I wasn't the only one cursed with the affliction. This disease could affect anybody. The person sitting across from you in the park could be a sufferer and you never could tell. The outward manifestations ~say the wearing of the *fáinne* ~ or even stranger still, the sight of somebody reading an Irish-language book in public ~ these were in no way a reliable guide as to who had the Irish disease or not. Just because you liked Irish or could speak it ~ or even if you let on that you could speak it; none of these traits were indicative of a full-blown obsession, the utter dependence that is characteristic of the true Irish-language addict.

The true addict was hooked, a person who couldn't get out of bed without inhaling every single breath of the lan-guage, every syllable, song and idiom every uttered, every adjective and noun. Do I really need to go any further? Do I need to drag in the Subjunctive Tense, the Vocative Case and all the rest of it? You get my drift.

Anybody who joined *Gaels Anonymous* was like this. Every pore of their being reeked of Irish. They ingested it and excreted it every moment of the day; they breathed it in with every breath that they took from cradle to grave. It was their very blood and sweat.

And what had driven us to that clinic in the end? Did we hope for a complete transformation, a cleansing or catharsis ~ did we expect to find a cure for our affliction, a cure as complete as it would be miraculous?

Not at all. All we wanted was to recover some form of equilibrium in our lives. A new balance to our days, some way of controlling the obsession with Irish that tormented us from morning to night ~ and through the night even. We sought, simply, to withdraw (somewhat) from our compulsive behaviour in relation to Irish. Without achieving some form of balance, every day of our lives would be a form of one-pointedness; we might even be obsessed for all eternity.

It might be a gradual process, requiring patience and fortitude, but we had to undergo it; there *was* another life out there; there was a life that lay outside the Irish language and we *had* to find it. A difficult process; take it from me. Incredibly difficult. Beyond belief. Almost impossible.

Some people found it more difficult than others, as you would expect, of course. None of us were under any illusions. We all knew that most of us would never achieve a real sense of inner peace. Our addiction was too strong; we couldn't wriggle out of the iron hold that the sweet Irish language had over us; we had gone too far already and it was too late for any real turning back. We were chronic cases; it was as simple as that. Reaching out to phrases and attitudes typical of the Anglosphere only made us look and sound ridiculous in the eyes of the world and in our own eyes.

75

When did we first realize that we were infected with the Irish language disease? That was one of the questions we tried to answer during group therapy sessions. Here are a few responses to this question as provided by some of the patients:

"When I first read a poem by Cathal Ó Searcaigh. I was completely enslaved from that moment onwards."

"I was at Irish College one summer when I felt a strange telepathic connection between myself and Patrick Pearse. It was right outside Pearse's Cottage that I got my first kiss."

Here's my response: My father had a copy of Dinneen's *Irish-English Dictionary*. Unknown to me, he too was an addict. Even my mother was unaware of his addiction. Nobody knew that he was addicted, not even other Irish-language enthusiasts. I myself was a teenager when I first began reading Dinneen – my father's copy. (God rest him.) I've been taking Dinneen ever since. I get my fix regularly. I always have it by my bed. I would give up life itself before weaning myself off Dinneen. Dinneen is life. Every time I use the dictionary, I feel some sort of mysterious connection with my father; every time I read the words that he marked...

Words like *buarach bháis, seicimín, ullastráth, móg.* Those words have multiple effects on me. They give me the shivers. I utter therm as sacred mantras. They are my prayers, my poems. Trips. Did my father have the same type of trips? He had marked pairs of words that had appealed to him: "*manglam bog:* an untidy armful of hay" and "*manglam dod:* a morning croon while preparing breakfast". Hundreds more. Where on earth would you get the likes of it?

Here's Hiúdaí's response: "I'm not trying to be a smart-ass, but I really can't remember a time when I was not completely and utterly addicted to Irish. I fully accept the theory of reincarnation. I was here before. I was a Gael. I lived through Cromwell's time. I saw what happened. Unfortunately I didn't live long enough to make any impression on that realm of existence. I didn't get a chance to be brave, to resist. And so I promised myself there and then that I would return. And here I am. And I can tell you one thing. I won't let a day go by in this present life of mine without speaking Irish, even if that means speaking to myself! Having said that, I would like to learn how to take a break from it, at times, without actually giving it up."

"Hang on a minute now! That won't do at all", interrupted the therapist on hearing this. "Reincarnation is it? Pull the other one! That's a load of old codswallop. That's just an excuse not to deal with your addiction. Now tell us straight. When did Irish take a stranglehold on you?"

"I've been addicted to Irish since the day I was born," said Hiúdaí. The therapist emitted a long, weary sigh. How can I best describe that particular therapist? She was one of those types – she was like the cat in that old saying: "'I've met you before,' as the cat said to the boiled milk." That's the type she was. One of those people who are tired before they are born. She had heard it all and seen it all before – according to herself, that is. An ignoramus if there ever was one! She hadn't a word of Irish. No interest in the language, no respect for it. How could she begin to understand how the likes of myself and Hiúdaí could be addicted to all the nuances and flavours of Irish? She could never comprehend the hit we got from something as simple as *bean* (woman) turning into the plural *mná*. Alchemy. Magic. Music.

In fact, she was reluctant to acknowledge that a condition such as ours existed at all; she was in denial. (How did she expect to cure us?). The disease exists and continues to exist and I'm living proof of it – ever since the

tests in Blackrock Clinic all those years ago. A news story which made headlines all over the world but like many such stories it has been largely forgotten today. For those who never heard about it, here's the gist:

Firstly, I was asked to read an extract from an English-language book after which they gave me a brain scan. *The Conscience of the Rich* by C. P. Snow. I remember the extract very well as I've read it quite often since:

As soon as I got back to London after that week-end, Ann asked me to dine with her. Once more she took me out in luxury, this time to the Ritz. I took it for granted, going out with her, that the waiters would know her by name: I was not surprised when other diners bowed to her. As usual, she set herself out to buy me expensive food and wine...

Once I had finished reading, I was directed into a machine (which looked like some kind of spacecraft) for a brain-scan. They found no trace of any endorphins in my system. Not the slightest. I was completely impassive and unmoved after reading Snow; not a flicker of excitement registered itself. I was taken out of the spacecraft and given a glass of water. Next thing, the nurse handed me a copy of *Eachtraí Phinocchio – The Adventures of Pinocchio*. It was Pádraig Ó Buachalla's version of the story, straight from the Italian. I opened page 27 and read the following:

Nuair a shrois Pinocchio an tráigh d'iniúch sé an fharraige go géar, ach má dhein ní fheacaigh sé Míol Draide ná éinní mar é. Bhí an fharraige chomh sleamhain le gloine.

"Cá bhfuil an Míol Draide?" ar seisean lena chom-rádaithe.

"Ní foláir nó tá scroid bheag aige á chaitheamh,"
arsa duine acu agus é ag gáirí.

"Ní dóichí rud a dhein sé ná é féin a chaitheamh
sa leabaidh chun greas beag a chodladh," arsa
duine eile, agus sceart sé ar gháirí.

Thuig Pinocchio go rabhthas tar éis bob a bhual-
adh air. Ní dheaghaidh san síos rómhaith leis agus
duairt sé go teasaí:

"Cad 'na thaobh díbh an cleas san a imirt orm? Ní
fheicimse go bhfuil aon tsulth ann."

"Tá, agus sulth go tiubh," ar siad san d'aon
ghuth...

I would have gladly continued reading all day and all
night. Back into the machine I went for another brain scan.

This time my brain was hopping with endorphins. I was
on fire, man. They could be spotted everywhere on the
scan, those merry little endorphins; buzzing through me,
zipping out from the pituitary gland and making their
delightful way into my spinal cord. A wonderful sight to
behold, ecstatic endorphins jumping for joy, all across the
surface of my brain. It was the use of that beautiful word
"sulth" that really kicked everything off, I think, rare as it
is to have that particular "t" softened by the "h"!

They did further tests on me and on a good many other
patients also. Funnily enough, it was Munster Irish that
induced the endorphins. Other dialects did practically
nothing for me. In the heel of the hunt, I was sent off to
another clinic for treatment. I was expelled from there,
however, when two volumes of the Irish of County Clare,
Caint an Chláir, were found hidden under my pillow. I
never returned to that clinic or any other clinic again
although I'm still a registered member of *Gaels Anony-*
mous. I follow the organisation's progress closely and I'm

always thrilled to hear of new developments in the field, the opening of a new branch in Singapore or Shanghai, for example.

Isn't it a strange one too? Clare Irish is dead for years and yet whenever I read a few sentences from *Caint an Chláir* the hairs stand up on the back of my neck and the endorphins go mad inside me.

I mentioned earlier that I came across my father's copy of Dinneen's *Dictionary* when I was still a teenager. This discovery confirmed for me that my father was very seriously addicted to the Irish language and how he managed to keep his addiction hidden from others is a mystery. After his death, I ransacked his library to see whether I could find deeper clues to his personality. I carefully scanned another dictionary, Ó Dónaill's, to see what it could tell me about him. He had only marked one word in the entire dictionary as it turns out – the word "canúnaí": *person interested in, addicted to dialect.* He had underlined the word "addicted" twice and placed a question-mark next to it on the margin of the page.

That question-mark haunted me for years. What did my father mean by the question-mark? Was it the definition of the word "canúnaí" that intrigued him or something far more profound? Was it his own existence he questioned, a secret life kept hidden from the world?

– Translated from the Irish by Mícheál Ó hAodha

Kaddish

The odd nightmare apart, Larry had never revisited boarding school. Strange, then, that he should agree to attend the reunion of past pupils of Carraig Pheadair, or Kerrickfeather, its official name.

Of the forty pupils who sat for the Leaving Certificate examination in 1979, he knew that two of them had gone on to receive their eternal reward; one of them, a very promising rally driver, had died in a crash. The other man had died of a heart attack. There was some talk of suffocation during an act of auto-eroticism.

There would be a huge meal. Perhaps to compensate for the pig slurry, as his friend Jack called it, pig slurry dished out during six years of incarceration. Wine would be consumed. Some fine wines, even. Not the thin altar-wine he had often purloined after serving Mass for that dotty old priest, Father Lonergan. They would spend the night in the same dormitory where they had once slept as school-boys. And look out at the same stars? The current generation had gone home for the Christmas holidays. The dormitory used to be called Siberia. Larry expected the heating to be set some degrees higher for past pupils.

Joxer, the lad who had once slept next to him, had once owned a plastic statue of the Virgin Mary, filled to the brim with "holy water". All you had to do was unscrew the head for a swig of pure vodka.

Of the thirty-eight souls still alive, seventeen turned up. The Angelus bell rang out across the tennis courts, the same as before, out across the playing fields towards the cold boundary walls. Some of them were even singing that silly old college song:

We're the boys from Kerrickfeather
We play hard – whatever the weather...

Larry never sang it. Because of this he was marked out as stand-offish, aloof.

The President, Father Edwards, welcomed them with the look of someone pretending to recognize your face or think of your name. Larry had to shake his hand.

"Larry," Larry mumbled.

"Of course it is! Good man! Welcome back, Harry!"

Father Edwards had hardly changed, a little more baldier, perhaps? It was Larry's fellow past-pupils that had aged. A few were beyond recognition. Old men. What wars had they been in?

Where was Jack Prendergast? Had he bothered to come at all? Would they recognize each other?

Grace Before Meals was said. The words came back to them, as though it were only yesterday, as though none of them had ever left school. Voices he hadn't heard in years, gestures he hadn't seen...

Bottles of wine were opened and the first course was served. Vegetable soup. The windows steamed up and soon he could no longer see the sun going down behind the wood. Larry felt trapped. He felt awkward, too, hearing just snatches of the rowdy exchanges.

"Can't complain... you know... yeah, I own two garages now... how about yourself?"

"Two daughters and one son..."

"I live in Foxrock..."

"We sent the son to Belvedere..."

"Do you remember Barry? Some character he was."

Explosions and spurts of laughter.

"Joxer's pissed already ~ would you look at the state of him!"

"Who? Oh, that eejit. I heard he ended up in Dubai. What? Don't ask me what's he's doin'. Screwin' the Arabs..."

An hour went by. One or two windows were opened. Outside, in the open car park, a light frost had fallen It glittered in the moonlight on the cars of the ex-pupils, a Jaguar here, a Volvo there, two Mercedes.

Larry couldn't concentrate on anything that was being said on either side of him. He found it well-nigh impossible to muster a laugh. The main course was served.

Ghosts, that's what they were. There's Jack Prendergast over there! He winked at Larry. Wouldn't you think ~ they hadn't seen each other until now ~ wouldn't you think that after all they had been through those long years ago... and just a wink of recognition? Wouldn't you imagine he'd get up from the table and walk over to Larry. Shake his hand or even place a hand on his shoulder? Hadn't they been the best of friends? Hadn't they written to each other on and off for five years ~ six years even ~ after leaving Kerrick- feather? And then? Then what happened? Nothing. Not a Christmas card even. Wouldn't you think he'd come over and say "Shalom!" like in the old days?

A tightness in his throat. Larry looked at the roast potatoes, the lamb, the peas. The mint sauce. He felt slightly queasy. "Pass the jug of water, please," he said to the person beside him.

"Would you not go for a drop of vino? It's a grand Rioja this..."

"Wa~water!" croaked Larry. The fellow next to him stared at him momentarily.

As he sipped the water, he noticed those faces looking over at him from the wall: the faded sepia photographs. Past-presidents of the college, a bishop or two, rugby heroes, a patriot here and there. In the corner, all alone, Christ on his Cross.

There were trophies and cups all along the surrounds of the refectory, mainly for rugby. It's not that he hated it as a sport, as some did. It's just that he and Jack had made a conscious decision not to be part of the crowd, neither to play Gaelic games nor what were sometimes called "foreign" games (not foreign to Kerrickfeather, of course). A decision that hadn't made life easy for them.

Back then, you weren't liked ~ by other pupils or by teachers ~ if you were different. To have a mind of your own made you a source of suspicion. The word "Queer" was scrawled on Jack's locker and "Poof" on Larry's at one stage. This was solely because they were more interested in the few fringe activities that were on offer ~ the debates, the tennis ~ than in rugby, the official religion of the college. No attempt had been made to discover who the graffiti offenders might have been, something which led Jack and Larry to believe that the authorities were part of the conspiracy.

Dessert was served. Larry recognized it as merely a slightly superior version of what was once offered here, so many years ago. He knew he couldn't eat it.

Neither he nor Jack had ever cheered on a rugby team. "The product of garrison culture!" Jacj liked to proclaim. They couldn't give two hoots about *esprit de corps*, a phrase that cropped up a little too often, they thought. They imagined that they were in a concentration camp and that instead of *Arbeit Macht Frei*, the words *Esprit de Corps* were posted over the gate. For a while, they even pretended to be Jews and greeted each other surreptitiously

104136

with "Shalom" and the like. They stamped numbers on each other's wrists. Jack used to call Larry the Chief Rabbi. Whenever it was pork for dinner, they'd hand over their share to some poor hungry devil and make do with the potatoes and vegetables.

Larry's stream of thought was interrupted by the sound of the bell. The President got to his feet: "Coffee will be served presently. I would like to take this opportunity to congratulate you all. We are very proud of you, all of you. Clearly what you learned here in Kerrickfeather and from our *esprit de corps* has not been wasted on you..." Twaddle!

Larry needed to stretch his legs. A few had left the refectory in search of fresh air. He went out and stood next to his car. He took out a packet of Silk Cut from his pocket. Someone behind him was jabbering into a mobile. More people emerged. He could see their breath in the air.

"Shalom!" came a voice from behind him.

He turned around. It was Jack.

"Still smoking, I see?" He gave him a toothy grin.

"Yeah... Jack." He offered him a cigarette. Jack refused with a wave of his hand.

"Don't smoke any more."

The sounds of the night. The smell of drink. Somebody throwing up. Cursing himself.

"How's the Chief Rabbi been all these years?" A quiet laugh.

Larry rolled up his sleeve a little. He bared his wrist.

"Jaysus, Larry – you can't be serious!"

"I'm the same as I always was," said Larry. He turned from Jack and looked sourly at an amorphous cloud that was about to swallow the moon.

– Translated from the Irish by the author

Bird Clan

I have to apologize to everyone (though saying sorry is not really adequate). I apologize to my parents, firstly. To relatives. To my fellow school-mates. To the police. The neighbours. To anybody else who was worried about me – or was out looking for me. There was no other solution to my predicament. No other way out of the situation. I had no option but to leave the world.

There were posters everywhere, I'm sure. Not that I saw any of them myself. They were in train stations and in police stations. On every street and corner. I'm not sure which photo of me they used, or what information about me they included. Not sure what they said about me in the newspapers either.

My age?

Hair colour?

Colour of eyes?

Last sighting?

Myself and seven others had gone missing. Maybe there were images of all eight of us on television? Were some of us spotted on a security camera in some shop or other? A big reward for information on our whereabouts?

Such a reward would have been offered in vain.

Other than the eight of us who made up the Bird Clan, no one knew where we were. No one knew whether I was alive or dead although there were plenty of rumours doing the rounds, I'm sure.

We'd been taken hostage by aliens and whisked away on a spaceship somewhere. Crazy rubbish like that! The reality was different. I spent a full year below ground – in the sewers, in the bowels of the earth. And I didn't get any certificate, diploma or degree for my troubles either. What I did get was something much more valuable in the end. The key to life.

There were eight of us altogether. Ten initially. Two were given wings early on. Permission to fly.

And it all began with a simple leaflet. A leaflet handed to me one day. The most significant event of my life – and it all began with a leaflet. Strangely enough, I can't remember the person who gave it to me. I remember a pale hand reaching out and giving me the leaflet, but that's all. I never saw his face. It was a dullish night in autumn.

A heavy fog came down as I stood outside a disco – I *do* remember that much. And I still have that leaflet. The one that changed my life. I don't need to read it ever again because the words are etched on my mind. They always will be:

You do *know that this country is corrupt, that the world itself is rotten to the core. You* DO *know that, don't you? Neither you nor anyone else can do anything about it. What could* YOU *do to change this? Nothing.*

That was it. That was the message. Blunt and straight to the point. There was nothing particularly attractive about it, was there? Not in the beginning anyway. To tell you the truth, I didn't pay much attention to it at first. I don't know how it didn't end up in the bin there and then, to be honest. It did have a fancy logo at the top; maybe that was why I didn't discard it? It was a picture of a sea eagle, a salmon in its clutches. Further down, at the bottom of the leaflet, was the following:

www.fiolar.org

Fiolar, of course, is the Irish for an eagle. I didn't bother enquiring about it for a long time. Sure, I took out the leaflet from time to time and had a quick look over it. Who might they be, I wondered. One of those strange sects we hear of from time to time? Or a band of eco-warriors? The words written on the leaflet went round and round in my mind until, eventually, curiosity got the better of me.

I checked out the website. I loved it straight away. I make no bones about it. I was hooked. Mesmerized. Why I can't explain. Some kind of emptiness in my life, I suppose? I got in touch with them, whoever they were. Then I packed my bag and hit the road. I didn't say anything to anyone else about it, said goodbye to no one. I left my family behind. Left the good people of Ireland behind, full stop.

I found myself accepted into a new family. The Bird Clan. I went underground, went to live in the dark world that lies beneath us. It wasn't entirely dark in that world below, however. For example, I was convinced I would be one of the youngest people living there. I was mistaken. At least half of the clan were around the same age as me.

The leader was a bit older than the rest of us, that is true. In his early twenties, a tall athletic type. He had brown piercing eyes and sported a funny-looking moustache. He wore his golden hair long, brushed back in a great sweep. At first glance, he was what you might call refined-looking and energetic. He was one of those types that you took your time figuring out.

"Let us welcome him," were the first words I heard him utter in my direction. He was definitely referring to me. He stood there, erect, in a military coat. Russian Army attire. One of those coats that you could pick up very easily in flea-markets some years ago. They were great for keeping you warm. Funnily enough, the temperature in the sewers always remained the same.

"My first duty is to assign you a new name," he announced. "From now on, we'll call you *Gealbhan*, Sparrow."

The buttons on his coat were gleaming brightly. I could see the reflection of the bonfire in them. The leader had a pleasant voice, fine and clear. He had a swagger about him, a self-confidence which exuded from every pore. His own name suited him perfectly, *Fiolar* – the Eagle. Next thing, I heard a murmur from the Bird Clan. They were repeating my name, chanting it reverentially in a low whisper. *Gealbhan... Gealbhan...*

They held scented herbs aloft as they chanted. (God knows we needed them in that place!) Gently they shook the batches of herbs, over and back in the air. I could smell lavender and something else I didn't recognize. Thyme maybe? Later I was told it was sage.

These people had total faith in their leader, Eagle. This much was very clear; it was written on their faces.

Like me, each member of the group had been given the name of a different bird. This was a custom which wasn't explained to me at first. They were testing me, I knew. They wanted to know whether I would adapt myself unquestioningly to their customs and habits or whether I would query the Clan's traditions, their ways.

I knew that I had much to learn, they told me so – provided I was willing to learn. Some of the teachings would be imparted in a non-verbal fashion, they also said. That came as a bit of surprise, I have to admit.

There were a whole host of other things which were never explained to me while I was there. In time I learned what they were and what they meant and that I had to learn from experience, from observation and not from the mouths of others. Indeed, by the time I'd completed my apprenticeship, I understood certain things that had completely bewildered me in the beginning. Needless to say, had I mentioned any of this to anybody outside the Clan they'd give me a funny look and say something like: "You've a great imagination. God bless you." These were aspects of life that were beyond the comprehension of any normal person.

What a great welcome I got when I first arrived on the scene. Everybody shook my hand and Eagle spoke:

"Let us remind our new friend ~ Sparrow ~ why we are here and what our mission is. You", he said, pointing to one of the Clan. "You explain it to him," he commanded.

The individual he had selected spoke as follows:

"I am Magpie. We all live in the sewers because we consider this place cleaner and more pure than the world above ground. The world up there is rotten in every way. The planet as a whole is in an awful state. Down here we don't bother reading newspapers or watching television ~ and if you bothered to follow the news you can be sure that it would be the same old story one week after the next. A war here. The threat of war there. Poverty. Famine. Oppression. Racism. Environmental destruction. The disappearance of all privacy. Threatened peoples, places, and languages. The very future of the planet is in danger."

"Fair play to you," Eagle said to Magpie. Eagle had just the trace of a smile around the corners of his mouth.

"Anyone want to add to that?"

Someone else spoke up then.

"My name is Swan. We are always learning new things here. Stay here with us under Eagle's protection and you can't go wrong."

I thanked Swan for his kind sentiments. Just then a girl put up her hand.

"Stand up, Robin," said Eagle.

She did as she was asked.

She had a small stutter in her voice. It came and went.

"J–j–just to ssay that Sparrow shouldn't for a moment worry that he will die of hunger here or anything."

A titter passed through the Bird Clan.

"Go on... Robin," said Eagle.

"There's p–plenty of f–f–food in Ireland. We live off the leftovers that are thrown out of the restaurants and cafés. And we often can't work out for the life of us why such-and-such a piece of fish or bread, or vegetable was thrown out in the first place. Most of the time this leftover food is as good, if not better, than what we were used to at home in our previous existence. We only scavenge outside the best joints. No fast food here! Last night we had s–s–swordfish and asparagus soup for our supper. The swordfish is a very tasty fish, Sparrow. But we sometimes have to test it for mercury."

She sat back down in her seat again. How do they test it for mercury, I asked myself.

"Anyone got anything else they'd like to get off their chest?" asked Eagle. He looked around at everybody. "Right so! Sparrow and Robin are in charge of preparing the food tonight. Swan is down for the washing up."

I looked over at Swan. His head was bowed in obeisance. No matter what duties we were assigned, I never saw anybody complain. Not once, during all the time I was there. I looked over at Robin. She looked back at me.

"And now we'll have two hours of silence," announced Eagle.

Such periods of silence were not unusual. It was usually two hours of silence per day; more if Eagle thought it necessary. In fact Eagle considered the endless and deafening talk that characterized the world above to be a major aspect of its impure nature. "Practise silence," was his mantra. "Practise silence and in doing so make recompense for all the stupid chatter of humanity ~ your own ridiculous chatter included."

There was never a gig out of anyone during the period of silence. The occasional cough, but that was about it. The odd rumble from the depths of the sewers.

Next thing I got a dig in the side from Robin. It was time for us to go off in search of food. Eagle was standing at the mouth of the sewer as we headed off. Just before we set off on our journey, he whispered something into Robin's ear. He spoke in a language I didn't understand.

What a beautiful feeling it was to fill my lungs with that lovely fresh air again!

I followed Robin wherever she went. She didn't look up or down, her eyes were completely focused on the path below. It was as though she were hiding from something or that she was afraid someone might recognize her. Funny. Her appearance had changed so much that her own mother probably wouldn't have recognized her!

I thought of my parents for a moment. They would be worried sick about me by now. Robin raised her wing slightly, indicating that I should follow her. I followed her down a dark laneway below. We arrived at the back door of a café. Robin had that intense look on her face as always, her head bent low like some bird intently foraging for worms.

We scavenged our way through the various bins here and there and it was indeed incredible how much beautiful food had been thrown out. We found enough sandwiches to fill five boxes. Then we set off again as quickly as we could. Robin pointed to the path beneath us again as indicating to me that I too should keep my head down. A police woman spotted us as we flew past and I was sure that she would hail us for questioning.

"We were lucky there," I said to Robin.

"H–h–how do y–y–you mean?" Robin stuttered.

"I was sure she was going to question us or call us in for suspicious behaviour."

"No. N–n–not at all," said Robin. "She didn't even see us."

"What?"

"Remember what Eagle said just before we left the sewers?"

"Yes, I was curious about that ever since we set off on our trip. That strange litany he spoke into our ears. I hoped it wasn't a shopping list. I didn't understand a single syllable."

"Eagle is a polyglot. He loves ancient languages in particular. He has an in-depth knowledge of Sanskrit and Old Irish. And he loves the L–l–language of Birds, a language as m–m–mellifluent as waterfall music. He's very fond of the tongues of the various elements. The wind rising up, say! Don't be talking! He goes cracked after the language of the wind. What you heard him utter in our ears that time was a charm. A prayer, if you will. It was the Charm of Invisibility that we heard that time, Sparrow. You don't have to bother holding your head downwards all the time, as if you were trying to hide. The truth is that nobody can see us anyway. S–s–seriously! Only other birds see us, others in the Clan."

Just at that very minute, a pigeon looked over at me. I looked back.

I spent the rest of the journey home deep in thought. I was meditating on what Robin had told me. Could this invisibility business be true? Did it make any sense at all?

We reached the sewers again. Robin warned me to stay alert in case anyone spotted us. Then she laughed out loud when she saw the look of consternation on my face. She had played another one of her tricks on me.

"Don't worry. You don't have to hide your head! Like I told you, we have the charm on our side. The Charm of Invisibility. Not a sinner can see us. Down we go now."

"There aren't any rats down here, are there?" I asked Robin.

No sooner were the words out of my mouth but a rat passed me by, his head tucked beneath him as he ran. Clearly, the Clan didn't pay much attention to the rats: that or both groups had learned to live side-by-side as happy neighbours. Or maybe the rat didn't see us – who knows?

It was hard to tell what age Robin was. Fourteen maybe? She had one of those freckled faces which made it difficult to tell – her face and nose all spotted and speckled. She wasn't one for too much chat either. She'd let a flood of talk out of her and then dry up. Not quite a flood. When she spoke it was in a halting voice as if she was thinking about every word she said before saying it. Slow and deliberate.

All in all, she was a decent and quiet-spoken sort of a bird. You know the type I mean. She kept her own small corner of the sewer very clean, as neat as a new pin. The only things she didn't disturb were the spiders and their webs. She wouldn't destroy a spider's web for gold or silver.

There was many a day in that first year of my apprenticeship when I asked myself why was it that I had decided to join this little community below ground. Was it written in my fate from the beginning? To tell you the truth, I was half-afraid of the other birds for a good while, in the beginning especially. This anxiety actually stifled me for a while. I doubted myself too, you can be sure I did. I had as many doubts about myself as I had about the Clan.

One afternoon Owl visited me without any warning. It was uncanny the way he arrived that day, out of the blue.

It was as if he had been reading my mind and had sensed my anxieties and doubts.

"Sparrow," says he to me, "don't be worried in the slightest. There is hardly anyone here who hasn't had doubts at some stage or another, everybody goes through the dark night of the soul. To have doubts is perfectly natural! It does us no harm in the greater scheme of things. To-whit, to-whoo!" and off he went.

Strangely enough, the most anxious night I spent there was that first night when Robin and I returned from our foray in search of food above ground. As we taxied down into the sewer with lunchboxes full of sandwiches, I felt strangely feral and animal-like. I'll never forget that feeling, all those eyes shining upwards at us as we came into land. They sparkled in the dark, all those sets of eyes, those gleaming orbs. They were like something I had never seen before ~ magic crystals that had remained buried for a thousand years and now revealed themselves in the light.

We cooked the food on a kerosene stove. Then ate it with our hands.

"Hunger is good sauce," said Swan to me.

He tore off a bit of what he was eating and threw it to a baby rat he kept as a pet.

Curiously, I never saw any close friendship develop that year between any pair of birds in the Clan. It was as if they were all independent entities. They all respected each other a great deal, this much is certain. But that is as far as it went.

Serious relationships were forbidden in the sewers.

Eagle was preparing us for something else, some great project the aims of which were grander and more ambitious. We were in training for a relationship with reality which was deeper and more intricate than we had ever known. An intimate relationship with the Universe ~ as he himself informed us. None of us understood too well what he meant by this new relationship, neither did we question it much either.

We didn't laugh a whole lot down there, to tell you the truth. Having said that, we were never gloomy or depressed. We knew that patience was of the essence, that Eagle was moulding us slowly but surely in preparation for this new state of being. Silence shaped us for the future.

Even as we slept, he was preparing us. So Magpie told me anyway. We weren't short of entertainment. The truth is that we were on edge with excitement. We were waiting for... what? It is difficult to put into words what it is we were waiting for. How to describe it – we were new-born birds awaiting the first flight.

One might think that such an environment would have brought out the primitive in me or that I would regress to some earlier state of nature. Nothing could be further from the truth. Where there had once been chaos, my life was now ordered. I felt my mind and will become stronger by the day. The same was true of the rest of the subterranean company.

Everybody had developed new forms of self-discipline or self-actualization.

It came as a surprise to me I have to admit.

"As soon as the first flickers of dawn come into the sewers, I'm up and at it," Owl admitted one day. "I wasn't like that when I lived up above, I can tell you!

When I lived up there, the devil himself wouldn't have dragged me out of bed in the morning."

"I wash my hair regularly now," said Magpie. "And look at my fingernails. They've never been more clean!"

Slowly but surely a new dignity and grace became apparent in each of us, that much was clear. A complete transformation really! Even the way we moved around was dignified. It was in our walk and in our hop. It was in the way that we took wing. Soon, this new way of being characterized all our actions. It was there in the way we related to one another, the way we communicated. We spoke to each other and our voices were polite, gentle even.

The smallest most insignificant thing now brought me happiness. I remember looking over at Magpie one day and watching the way he settled himself on a bundle of rushes. The way he perched on the rushes, the way he arranged them carefully beneath him. There was something kingly and gracious about the whole operation. I felt a special bond of solidarity with the whole Clan now, it was a form of love. We were all united as one, and if one of us was hurt in some way then we would all feel the pain.

The influence of Eagle became greater on us all the time. For the first time in my life, I understood what it was to have an aura of dignity surrounding my being. I knew what it meant to have good manners, how necessary they are for a human being to live well. They make life easier for everyone, simpler, more effective and more graceful too. What are good manners except learning to forget about oneself? The needs of the *other* person are paramount.

In the sewers this way of living was not just an ideal. It was a given aspect of our daily interactions. We accepted it as the normal course of events.

"Our only duty is to survive as a self-sufficient group," Eagle said to me one day. "If we all think as one – as a unit – then we will function as one. Let us not allow personal feelings come between us and this idea; with love comes jealousy and then such concepts as "yours" and "mine". We have left all that behind us now. The love I speak of is not the love of tribe and parish, of native land. No! The only thing necessary now is that love which encompasses every inch of this entire planet. This is the only thing that is required now. Do you understand what I am saying?"

I told him that I did.

I needed a change of clothes badly.

"Wear the same clothes," said Eagle, "wear them until they are so worn that they fall from your bones. When that happens, we will send out two of the Clan to buy you new clothes. Seagull and Thrush are normally the ones we send out. They are the best at procuring garments."

It was two months later that I got a change of clothes; unfortunately, the trousers were too large for me, the jacket too narrow.

"You look like a scarecrow!" Owl said when he saw me. I didn't care one way or the other. It made no difference to me. Sure, the only people who would see me were the Clan and they loved me for who I was, not for the clothes on my back.

I was still prey to the odd bout of insecurity and self-doubt. I'd wake up stressed in the middle of the night, only to ask myself: "Why don't I just get the hell out of here? Here I am, in the early bloom of youth, living in a sewer in the company of people whom I will never really fully know or understand." But one look at the others as they slept ~ (except for Eagle, that is, I never once saw him sleep) ~ and I knew that there was nothing I had left behind which could be better than this life. Eagle had definitely worked his magic on me, as well as all the others.

In much the same way as the Church assigned each day of the year to a different Saint, to too did Eagle name each day after a different Bird. He'd announce what day it was first thing each morning. Today is the "Day of the Crow", he'd say, and we had to sit in a circle then, cawing away in imitation of the crows ~ so much so that we were often hoarse by the end of the day.

Caw! Caw! Caw!

Caw! Caw! Caw!

If somebody had walked in on us there and then, what would they have made of us at all? You wouldn't have seen the likes of it in a film. Initially, I thought this bird imitation business was the stupidest thing ever. I thought (or part of me thought) it was completely crazy. I began to question myself:

"Who is Eagle really? Where did he come from? Is he some kind of a lunatic?"

Slowly but surely I became entranced by this chanting, however. Before long, I couldn't imagine anything more pleasant than those chanting and cawing sessions. I looked forward to them so much. Eventually, I considered it the sweetest sound in all creation. All those voices celebrating in unison until you no longer heard your own voice as a separate entity. It was as if your voice was carried on a great and celebratory wave, an eternal wave of sound more meaningful than words. I became very adept at imitating the various birds of the air and the sky. My progress was swift. Before long, I could make different sounds with my lips and my tongue, with my throat and even with my breast ~ each sound an accurate imitation of the characteristic calls of birds. This new-found skill gave me joy that was almost surreal in its intensity.

Were human beings once like this? I asked myself. Did prehistoric man have such a close bond with his environment that he could communicate with the deer and the eagle? And I felt a great pity for all those people in the world who were so disconnected from nature that birdsong was something completely alien to them.

I really felt deep compassion for the individual who would never know the plover from the snipe. How did Eagle have such a knowledge of bird music, all their songs and stories? He could even sing the song of certain extinct birds, melodies that struck us dumb!

And when he gave his own call – the Eagle's whistle – you never heard anything quite like it, a divine echo all along the walls of the sewer, a sound so mysterious that it put the hairs standing on the back of your neck. And those who heard that whistle, their mind was made pure, their heart made forever new, no other thought drifting in us but how to renew the world above, save it from itself. When we heard that sound our hearts were filled with the mystery of life itself. And for this rebirth of the spirit, we gave Eagle thanks.

Before long I realized that Eagle was a font of knowledge not just on the speech of every species of Irish bird and many foreign birds besides – but also on the positive effects which birdsong could have on human beings. There was some strange link between the rhythms of birdsong and the regulation and movement of the human brain, the tides and waves of the mind.

In a strange way too, the *Caw! Caw!* that formed the harsh music of the crows was a form of physical regulation in the body. It affected our lungs and created a rhythmic circular form of breathing. It was as if with every cry of *Caw! Caw!* our lungs were being emptied of every stale breath that they had ever held. The deep percussion of the pigeons had a dreamy harmony all of its own. A half an hour of pigeon-chat and you found truth in every dream you had ever dreamt. It calmed us down, made us sleepy. We listened to twenty minutes of pigeon-music every night just before sleep. On waking, we imitated the lark in search of our morning mood. The delicate music of the cuckoo also brought a regular, cooling joy to our hearts.

Eagle always knew what music was appropriate to the hour. Imitating the blackbird was the best bet for anyone who was feeling sick whereas the seagull's cry was a great tonic for any of us who might be suffering from exhaustion or depression.

There was a noisy waterfall about four kilometres away and it was here that we went to wash ourselves, body and soul. Eagle claimed healing properties for the tumbling waters there.

"He who listens to the speech of the waterfall never suffers mental stress or strain," he once remarked.

Where did Eagle get all of his knowledge I wondered. Was he some kind of a druid or shaman? He was certainly a Master in his field, that much was certain.

"I've never once seen him angry," said Magpie one day.

"Me neither," said Swan.

My respect for Eagle grew with each day that passed. I no longer had any doubts about him. He was blessed with special powers and he was using them to protect and strengthen the Clan. Or had he another even grander plan in mind?

Once you had spent six months in the sewer, you were allowed to ask Eagle one question per month. You could ask more than one question provided each question related to the same theme. Once I had six months put in, I asked Eagle the following question:

"That tattoo on your hand. It's a salmon, right?"

"Yes. It sure is, Sparrow. The same salmon that you saw on that recruitment leaflet you were handed. It was I who handed you the leaflet by the way."

"I never saw you that day, Eagle."

"I know well that you didn't, Sparrow, my lad! Invisibility is necessary from time to time."

Invisibility. What was that? Was it a miracle? Or an illusion of some sort?

What was a particular source of fascination to me was the tattoo.

"What's the deal with the salmon anyway?"

"The old Irish word for a salmon is *eo*. And *eo* is the root of the word *eolas* or knowledge, *eolaíocht*, science, *eochair*, key. The sea-eagle captures the salmon in its talons. There is a symbolism here that is very old. Merlin and the druids, the Celts and the Picts – they knew about these things, the summit and the nadir."

I had been right all along. Eagle was a druid! Where had he accessed this arcane knowledge?

Robin assured me that he had been born that way – Eagle was born a druid. He had the gift of wisdom from the very first moment, from the cradle itself. What plan had Eagle in mind for us? (If he had a plan, that is.) That was the next question. I would have to stay in the sewer for another month before I could ask him that particular question.

After all, Eagle was a loner, a bird who kept to himself most of the time. The odd time he called out, alone, and you heard his whistle wherever you were. How to describe it? It was a whistle of wonder, a long thin whistle. The whistle of the eagle from the cliff-edge, the whistle of wind and of loneliness, the whistle of eternity. A month passed and I asked Eagle my question.

"You have a plan in mind for us Eagle, don't you?"

Eagle looked at me intently for a moment. He stared at me with those eagle eyes of his.

"What will happen is that you will be set free. Not that you aren't free to leave now of course, if you really want to. In the end you will all be free to go, that is the plan."

"When will that be?"

"When you are properly prepared for the journey. When you are ready to go. When you are all fully attuned and in complete harmony with your own nature. At the moment you are absorbing all of the wisdom and arcane knowledge that is necessary. Every day that passes here, you are further along the road of self-knowledge. Consciously or not, all of you are currently weaving the protective tapestry that is pure silence. And it is within this silence that the unique voice of each bird will come to be heard ~ Starling and Thrush, Swallow and Sandpiper, Cormorant and Lark ~ each voice unique and inimitable."

He stretched out his two hands then as if forming a set of wings.

"No other message is being promulgated here. In fact, the rules that we follow have little importance in the greater scheme of things. We have no particular gospel to disseminate, no special vocation to live out. When you are finished here you will know whom to call upon when help is required. You will know whom to call and when. And help will come to you, swiftly on the wing."

He looked at me and through me. He looked past me and then turned his gaze inwards upon himself.

"And it doesn't matter where in the world you find yourselves, you will be performing this Great Work. We fled the world and sought sanctuary underground in order to attune ourselves to those parts of us which required development. To be whole again. It is not possible to put this into words, to give it shape before the time comes. You will each face different obstacles and will have to adapt to whatever scenario presents itself. This is something that I

107

cannot predict in advance; it is the reason for your time of preparation, your formation. But here, take this, this will be useful to you when you find yourself in peril."

He blew into my left ear. I felt his breath on my neck. I shivered. He pulled away from me again for a moment.

"I have given you the spirit of the Vulture. It will be with you always."

We weren't always reliant on the detritus left over by the restaurants. Eagle would send us out sometimes to gather other types of food – nuts, berries and herbs. We often had to fly far away from home in search of other foods. Eagle was an excellent cook. Nettle soup was his speciality. He wasn't short of a sense of humour either: we used to eat shamrock on Saint Patrick's Day!

Once a month we had a Poetic Court. Although many of us would never have thought of composing a poem previous to this, we all made up our own verses, some of them funny, some of them sad and some of them downright strange. I'll never forget the poem Crow recited for us one day, a poem entitled *Dachau*:

> *Black as cinders*
> *The crows that fly over Dachau:*
> *The wings of their ancestors*
> *turned black in the smoke of the Holocaust.*
> *Cá! [Where?] Cá! [Where?] Cá! Where are they?*
> *Men, women and children...*
> *Black as cinders*
> *The crows that fly over Dachau*

One morning Eagle instituted a new schedule.

"It is time to teach the body what the mind has learned. Let us dance!"

He told us all to stand in a circle. Then he stood in the middle of us.

"Let us begin with the Peacock's Dance."

Carefully, he taught us each movement of the dance. Step by step. It came as a bit of a surprise, this incredibly slow dance of his. Not only did he dance with his feet. He danced too with his arms. His eyes! There was no part of him that was not dancing.

He called Robin over and they danced together. We couldn't but stare at the look of sheer ecstasy on her face; she was like someone whose heart could burst with happiness at any moment.

Eagle's wise teachings ~ taught through chant, dance and silence ~ gave us all great courage. I could see that he had moulded us so as to transcend our normal limitations. I knew that my period of apprenticeship was coming to an end. One day I went to talk with him ~ to thank him for all that he had done for me.

"Ireland will be grateful to you one day," I told him. "The entire world will thank you some day."

I said other things to him also, things that shall remain between the two of us forever. When I was finished, he wove a crown made of feathers and placed it on his head regally. Placing his finger in the centre of my forehead, he asked me to sing a special charm with him. The words I repeated were as follows:

Bhava sagara saba sukha gaya hai
(I am not afraid to travel across the ocean of life)

I felt an incredible surge of energy pass through my body. It coursed through my spine and reared up in me like a great and noisy tumult, a waterfall powering upwards! The damp walls of the sewers shimmered with the might of its invisible power.

"If sewer walls can appear this beautiful and heavenly, there is nothing in this great world that cannot be saved," I called out in ecstasy, my power of speech restored.

Tears poured from my eyes. Eagle removed a feather from his crown and placed it in my hair.

"Sparrow, gentle soul. Your wings are ready for their journey. Fly away now, the moment has finally come! Go! Fly!"

~ Translated from the Irish by Mícheál Ó hAodha

About the author

Gabriel Rosenstock was born in 1949 in Kilfinane, Co. Limerick. He is a poet, novelist, playwright, haikuist, and author/translator of over 170 books, mostly in Irish. First came to prominence as one of the INNTI poets at University College, Cork. Taught haiku at the Schule für Dichtung (Vienna), and the Hyderabad Literary Festival. A prolific translator of poems, plays, and songs, he also writes for children, in prose and verse, and is the Irish-language translator with Walker Éireann. Represented in *Best European Fiction 2012* (Dalkey Archive Press) and *Haiku in English: The First Hundred Years* (W. W. Norton & Co. 2013). *Books Ireland*, Summer 2012, says of his novel *My Head is Missing*: 'This is a departure for Rosenstock but he is surefooted as he takes on the comic genre and writes a story full of engaging characters and a plot that keeps the reader turning the page.' An Associate of the Haiku Foundation and a Charter Member of the Haiku & Tanka Society. *Where Light Begins* is a selection of haiku. *The Invisible Light* features haiku in Irish, English, Spanish, and Japanese with work by American master photographer Ron Rosenstock. *The Naked Octopus* consists of erotic haiku translated into Japanese by Mariko Sumikura and illustrated by Mathew Staunton (Evertype 2013). Rosenstock's selected poems, translated from the Irish by Paddy Bushe, is called *Margadh na Míol in Valparaíso/The Flea Market in Valparaíso* (Cló Iar-Chonnachta 2013). Among his awards is the Tamgha-I-Khidmat medal for services to literature.

Blog address: roghaghabriel.blogspot.ie